WEIRD HORROR

D1628293

No. 4

WEIRD HORROR 4
SPRING 2022

PUBLISHER
Undertow Publications
1905 Faylee Crescent, Pickering ON, L1V 2T3, Canada

Undertowpublications.com
WeirdHorrorMag@gmail.com

EDITOR
Michael Kelly

PROOFREADER
Carolyn Macdonell

LAYOUT
Courtney Kelly

OPINION
Simon Strantzas

COMMENTARY
Orrin Grey

BOOKS
Lysette Stevenson

FILMS
Tom Goldstein

COVER ART
Drazen Kozjan

COVER AND MASTHEAD DESIGN
Vince Haig

INTERIOR ART
David Bowman

SUBMISSIONS
undertowpublications.com/weird-horror-magazine

ISSUE 4   CONTENTS   SPRING 2022

Next Wave Horror, On Horror, by Simon Strantzas ... 4

Clowns at Midnight, Grey's Grotesqueries, by Orrin Grey ... 6

The Floating House, by J.F. Gleeson ... 9

Fever Girls, by Linda Niehoff ... 14

Camera's Eye, by Daniel David Froid ... 18

Arachnids in Your Bed: An Interactive Bedtime Story for Children—and Adults, by Sarina Dorie ... 26

Milk Teeth, by Annika Barranti Klein ... 29

Whenever it Comes, by Steve Rasnic Tem ... 40

Hurled Against Rocks, by Andrew Humphrey ... 43

Fields and Scatter, by Ashley Stokes ... 51

Sunder Island, by Derrick Boden ... 61

Figments of the Night, by Armel Dagorn ... 73

The Macabre Reader, Book Reviews by Lysette Stevenson ... 77

Aberrant Visions, Film Reviews by Tom Goldstein ... 82

Welcome to the new pulp! Weird Horror magazine is a venue for fiction, articles, reviews and commentary. Published twice yearly - Spring and Fall.

ON HORROR

CR&O

SIMON STRANTZAS

NEXT WAVE HORROR

I think we're in an exciting time for Horror right now—at the cusp of a radical shift in storytelling from what we've so far experienced—and there are real questions about what that divergence might mean if it happens (or if it doesn't happen at all) for the field's future.

There have thus far been two radical shifts in Horror fiction over its relatively short existence. Before you start regaling me with stories of Gilgamesh and how horror stories have always been with us, let me explain: Horror, as a genre, has existed since roughly the 1970s. Before this there were authors who wrote horror stories, but these were not necessarily classified as such at the time, and often were not the only sort of story these authors told. Pre–1970 (and increasingly true as one travels further back in time), authors were more likely to treat the horror story as simply one from a range of different story models they might draw from. It was only

around 1970, thanks to the success of books like *The Exorcist*, *The Other*, and *Rosemary's Baby*, that the horror story went from something that an author wrote to something that defined an author. To put it another way: we went from having authors who wrote horror stories to having Horror authors. These were the First Wave Horror writers.

These writers are considered "First Wave" primarily because they started writing after the 70s, and because they were the first to consider themselves (even temporarily) "Horror writers", but I'd argue they are also defined by the sort of stories they wrote. In many ways they were carrying on the traditions of those working before them—most popularly the California circle of writers like Matheson and Bradbury—and their aim was to explore different ways of telling a Horror story. What defines a Horror story? In this case it's what comes immediately to mind—notable tropes

such as evil children and twist endings. So much of what the wider public considers Horror was concretized by these writers, and arguably First Wave Horror remains the most popular form of horror story in the mainstream. We don't need to look further than the Horror Boom to see this is the case—never before or since was the Horror story so popular. And the simple fact that Stephen King continues to be a significant presence in literature and film fifty years later only further emphasizes the success of First Wave Horror.

Then, around the turn of the millennium, there was a shift, and we saw the rise of Second Wave Horror. Unlike writers from the first wave who grew up in a pre-Horror world, the Second Wave writers only knew a world that contained Horror...or, maybe more specifically, only knew a world where Horror was a major marketing category. During these writers' formative years the bookstore shelves were overflowing with Horror novels, and the multiplexes were stuffed full of Horror films. Second Wave Horror writers were steeped in Horror fiction, and when they finally came of age to write their own stories, they pulled from their vast, expansive, and life-long knowledge of the genre's workings. I'd argue that Second Wave Horror is in direct conversation with and a reaction to First Wave Horror. Because the basics of the genre had already been so thoroughly explored, what these Second Wave writers did was introduce a wider vision to Horror. Where influences were relatively constrained with the First Wave, with the Second writers began to look more broadly, taking their cues not from variations on the established tropes but from deeper, more metaphorical horrors. The most successful of these Second Wave writers found inspiration in the cosmicism of Lovecraft, the oneiricism of Aickman, the pessimism of Ligotti, to forge a new kind of Horror that was called "Weird Horror" for lack of a better way to separate it from the First Wave that preceded it.

We are in the twentieth year of Second Wave Horror, and I suspect we are nearing its end. As with the earlier First Wave, I think much of the ore in this sort of fiction has been mined, and we're about to experience another shift led by a new wave of writers who are likely already percolating up through the small presses. It makes sense if you consider that First Wave Horror also reached its peak at about twenty years before beginning to fade out. The biggest difference now is the world has changed tremendously over these last few decades, and the slow ramping down then ramping up at the end of the 90s is unlikely to happen again. Things move faster now, the respectability of Horror (as with all genres) has somewhat increased, and many of the walls that once kept young writers from some sort of readership have crumbled away. We're left with a world where there may not even be waves anymore but instead just a steady and constant onslaught of new writers and new kinds of work. A state of constant flux and noise, one that will be impossible to parse because it's so overwhelming. A world where everything that can exist will exist and all at once.

But, assuming it's not as dire as all that, what will constitute this next wave, this Third Wave of Horror? I suspect what we're about to see is the end of the narratives we've been so used to for decades. By which I mean the default straight white male narrative. I also think this potential next wave will reject the notion that Horror needs to be viewed through a solely Western lens. Just as Second Wave Horror writers redefined *what* Horror stories could be about; Third Wave Horror writers will redefine *who* they can be about. We're already seeing evidence of this sort of transformation in other genres, but Horror has always been more conservative the closer to the mainstream it gets, so changes take a bit longer to make themselves known. But trust that they will; that it's only a matter of time. We just need that one writer to catch the attention of the field to focus people on the undercurrent that's been swelling. It happened with Stephen King during the First wave and happened again with Laird Barron during the Second. I don't know who it will be during the Third, but no doubt they're out there now, writing stories, honing their craft, and in no time at all they will bring a new and different way of interacting with Horror with them.

As I said: this is an exciting time.

GREY'S GROTESQUERIES

ᘓᘔᗞ

ORRIN GREY

CLOWNS AT MIDNIGHT: WHY SILLY ISN'T THE OPPOSITE OF SCARY

"There are no stranger bed-fellows than horror and humor."

In the newest edition of the classic D&D adventure *Curse of Strahd*, those words open the section that describes how using "a dash" of humor "provides a respite, giving horror a chance to sneak up on us later and catch us off guard."

It's just one of many examples of taking for granted a kind of unspoken consensus that funny is the opposite of scary. When we laugh at something, this common wisdom seems to assert, we take its power away. It's even become a trope, of sorts. Take the scene in *Harry Potter and the Prisoner of Azkaban* where Professor Lupin teaches the class about boggarts. Boggarts, it seems, take the shape of our greatest fear. And the methodology that the scene posits to combat that fear is to use a charm to trans-

form the boggart into something amusing, thereby literally taking its power to frighten away from it.

Though this maxim generally remains unspoken, I feel like it guides a lot of the creation of modern-day horror. Most artists, writers, filmmakers, and so on seem to strive assiduously to keep anything overtly goofy out of their horror material—at least, the ones who want to be taken seriously do. Instead, we get somber meditations on grief, or bloody and brutal depictions of ostensibly real-istic violence, and when there *is* humor, it is often winking and self-referential.

However, I am of the opinion that this old saw about goofy vs. scary actually misses the mark pretty widely and, as a result, horror creators who take it to heart, even unconsciously, are actually doing themselves and their work a grave disservice.

After all, things that are

intended to be goofy or silly definitely *can* be scary. Just ask any coulrophobe. Lon Chaney—senior, in this case—already knew it a hundred years ago. "A clown is funny in the circus ring," he is often quoted as saying, "but what would be the normal reaction to opening a door at midnight and finding that same clown standing there in the moon-light?"

Humor and horror, then, are not merely strange bed-fellows—they are practically two sides of the same coin. After all, we're as likely to laugh as scream when some-thing startles us; as likely to whistle or tell jokes as we pass by a graveyard as we are to keep silent in the hopes that nothing takes notice of our passing.

Solemnity may be one side-effect of fear, but so is levity. It's a way that we express our nerves, sure. Laugh at ourselves for our own (over) reactions to someone jumping out and saying "boo!" But it's also because what makes us laugh and what makes us afraid are separated by a razor's edge—and that razor can cut.

Some of the very best practitioners of modern horror know this and excel at walking the tightrope that turns silly into sinister—and sometimes vice versa. Take the work of perhaps the most celebrated modern horror mangaka, Junji Ito. Throughout his many twisted tales, there are countless scenarios that, on paper, sound utterly goofy yet, when rendered by him, become absolutely horrifying—in part precisely *because* of their goofiness.

"The Hanging Balloons," printed in English in Ito's *Shiver* collection from Viz, under the title "Hanging Blimp," is one good example. The premise is as simple as it is bizarre. After a girl commits suicide by hanging, balloons that look exactly like the heads of living people begin to appear in the sky, trailing nooses. They follow the person they resemble until they can catch them outside, at which time the noose slips around their neck and hangs them, dragging them into the sky.

The image of giant, disembodied heads floating around like balloons is unequivocally silly. Without the nooses, they could just as easily exist in a children's cartoon show. Yet in Ito's hands, that silly image becomes grotesque in the extreme.

You can find similar approaches to the silly and horrific at play in the bizarre horror vignettes of author Matthew M. Bartlett, or the viral internet video sensation "Too Many Cooks." Then there are the many social media ghouls of artist Trevor Henderson, best known as the creator of Siren Head, who has been repurposed into everything from video games to plush figures to party decorations.

Among Henderson's many popular creations are entities such as Cartoon Cat, a giant, well, cartoon cat that could have come straight out of the days of rubber hose animation—an era that, incidentally, produced more than its share of nightmare fuel in the name of "silliness."

It: Chapter One (2017)

In fact, it was Henderson who prompted me to write this column, when he tweeted, "For a monster to be scary it needs to be at least a little silly, otherwise it leans towards 'cool,' which is almost never scary, imo." The link between silliness and scariness was one that I had already been entertaining for a while, but what made this column congeal was the *other* nail that Henderson hit on the head. *Silly* isn't the opposite of scary; *cool* is.

Or, perhaps more accurately, one of the *many* experiences and phenomena that we mean when we use the word "cool," since "cool" is all-but meaningless. We use it to describe pretty much anything that we like. But it has another, more specific connotation. The kind you would use for John Wick or Batman or ninjas if you were a kid in America in the '80s. *Those* are the things that are the opposite of scary.

We see those things as aspirational—or maybe we only did when we were 12. We want to *be* those things, not be frightened by them. It's why you hardly ever see slashers doing spin kicks or driving sports cars. It's also (one small slice of) why *Halloween Kills* didn't work for me at all. That opening sequence, the one where Michael kills a whole screen full of firefighters in what looks like a video game cutscene? It makes him look cool. It's the scene that an action hero would get.

That's why Michael is scary in the original *Halloween*, where he kills a grand total of, like, five people, but he isn't scary at all in *Halloween Kills*, where he offs more than five times that number.

By then, he's become too "cool."

The Hanging Balloons (1998)

THE FLOATING HOUSE

☙❧

J. F. GLEESON

I did not like the floating house.

On only four occasions did I have to visit it. But I did not like it.

My father worked in a betting shop and on days when I was not at school he would sometimes take me on visits to people's houses. I do not know if they were explicitly related to his work in the shop; certainly in hindsight I recall nothing animus between him and the people he visited, and they were always friendly enough to him, and friendly enough to me.

The floating house was at the bottom of a thin long street with too many cars parked down it, all of which were crammed and bent, and it went on, downhill, and steeply, like an over-stuffed mouth full of too many teeth. On this street, the houses, while never ugly, leaned into each other tenuously.

The name of the particular house of which I speak does not perhaps betray its interior secrets: the house itself did not float.

The people inside it did.

There was a short gate between the low garden walls and a stunted path to the front door. I would look at the asymmetrical shingle and the potted plants. We would be greeted, each time, by the man who owned the house, who had too many teeth in his mouth, and when he smiled I saw a thin long street with too many cars that had tried to park on it. He would greet us, and take us through to the living room, where he and my father would talk and I would not be interested, and sometimes daytime television would be left on. The adults on the television would be sat around on couches talking very importantly, and very, very bo-

ringly. I would be even less interested in that.

My father and the man would not talk much to me, nor I much to them, on my part mostly as a result of that strange shyness that would heat on my face on meeting new teachers, new parents of friends, or even on coming across relatives we did not often see. I would do little more than sit about in the house unless I was colouring or scrawling, and as the adults spoke and my mind made their voices into water, the people would float about.

The people who floated about the house were quietly terrifying and I do not remember being so unnerved by any other thing in my young or adult life. My father and the man only once reassured me, on our first visit, telling me that it was all right, they were all right, there is nothing to be frightened of. They said it in that manner that is for children, the manner of sharing more of a private joke between themselves than being much bothered. The other times we visited, the people floating around were not much acknowledged.

The people who floated about the house did so without purpose and without direction, and drifted, not noticeably moving apart from their drift, moving as, if something in our universe must be compared to it, corpses might in space. They knocked against the door frames and the ceiling. They would, so very slowly, so very quietly too for they made no sound, drift in and out of rooms, up and down the stairs. My first close encounter came when I ascended to the upper floor to use the bathroom: I turned to find somebody floating up after me, and saw its alive eyes, and all of their alive eyes looked at nothing; its weightless sleeved arms knocked the walls gently and came away from them. Naturally I thought it came towards *me*, so I ducked and cried and ran back down to my father, who told me it was fine and gave me a packet of crisps. Quite oppositely to pursuing me about the house, that floating person had risen up the staircase.

I was, as you might well imagine, quite sick to see these floating silent bodies, though with some wonder I watched them when they brushed against the light fittings, caught and drifted about the ceilings. Like any child, I had often hung upside down off the sofa, imagining the room turned the wrong way around, walking on the ceiling and having to step over the tops of the doorways. To see these strangers though was an incorrect experience of that; a perversion of my very childish impression of *flying* as a magical thing. It was Peter and the Darlings who flew. It was the cartoons. It was I, in dreams, soaring though only then for paltry distances before I came back down; not even in night-time fantasies to be fully loose from the ground.

Occasionally before we left we would sit out in the garden, the man locking the door behind him, and if I had been sickened to be in the rooms with these ghouls, I almost brought back up my apple juice to be *outside*, to see them wash past the window *inside*, bobbing into other rooms that I could not see, rearranging themselves for surprise when we returned. There were perhaps five in total, though it is possible some were different on our different visits. The faces of only three I remember clearly; one in particular, which will become horrifically clear.

○

On the last of our visits, we arrived and stayed quite late, till it was in fact black out, though at least this later afternoon had meant children's television had made it onto the living room screen, though then off again, and as some news

or quiz or political show that bored me terribly churned on, I overheard the grownups talking about my staying the night in the floating house.

I right away became quite nervous, as sleeping was something with which I already had difficulty. I found it near impossible to drift peacefully off in the houses of my grandparents, or on holidays in the west or the north, or on holidays anywhere, and even in my home, if I were not asleep before my mother and father had stopped listening to the radio downstairs; if, that is, I were the only person left awake in a house, I could become very panicked and soak my pillows with tears.

My father and the man who lived in the floating house continued talking about my sleeping there. I had not been focused on the television in any case; with my back to the wall, I was alert to the potential comings and goings of the floating people, and indeed, a brush against the living room door and I saw one flow, half-figured in the dim hallway light, past us. Without interjection I listened to the comings and goings of the chat, and tied myself to any few words that suggested I would not have to stay, or that I could go back home with my father. To my dread this did not come to pass.

Father finally turned to me and told me, as I crunched through a packet of crisps that were shaped like animated ghosts, that I would need to stay the night here, and that the room was very nice, and that I'd quite like to stay wouldn't I. Used as I was not to speaking my thoughts but to pleasing anyone who asked anything of me, and used also to the wrung expression of my father's face when my mother would comfort me, as though my fears and hurts were an irritant to him, I said I would.

My father said a night-night to me, and a goodbye to the man, and left, and the man left me to sit in front of the television and whatever anonymity was on it, and though I was scared I had not the nerve to ask anything otherwise of the man, particularly as he scarcely interacted with me. At a certain point a whisking sound gave me a start, and I ended the evening tightened into a corner of the room, staring up at the woman who had floated into it; I could not quite see her as she was awash in blackness and the gauze off the television, though she seemed to be wearing a striped top, and she knocked mostly against the ceiling and the light fittings, and the top of the mirror above the mantelpiece. Her eyes lost their qualities in the dark, and gained new ones.

This seemed, as many things did at that age, to go on for a great many years, until the man came to show me to my room upstairs. It would have been a pleasant room, possibly, in the day, with a window that looked out on the garden and cerulean walls, though now there was a thick black blanket hanging over the window, and the room became, with the lights on, very flat and night-time, and with the lights off, very dark and full of sickness.

I was to sleep on the top of a bunkbed, and the man left me to myself and closed the bedroom door. A tiny, lost trapezoid of light showed that he had left the landing illuminated.

My immediate thought, with the lights out and the pit of silence, was that I did not know how they expected me to sleep. Panics I experienced at night in my own home came from great sweeping fears of what would happen to me at the end of my life, or of my parents' sudden vanishing, as though I had retained from infancy the habit to forget the existence of anyone not in the currently visible vicinity.

The lights were out in a very oppressive fashion, though I was so mentally oppressed by childish routines and rules in any case that I could not bring myself to switch them on. Besides which, a part of me did not want to brighten the shadow-packed corners.

The door was firmly shut, but I could not stop thinking about them: their eyes that rolled around though I had not seen them roll, drifting about with inhuman direction; the gazing float; floating into rooms without want, unable to escape them until some accident of air or wind or trajectory bounced them back out again. In the black I stared at the door, and following the man's footsteps into his own bedroom, the landing light went out also, and for there was not a single other sound in the house, I listened for the skims of people floating in the other rooms and halls.

I fell at some stage to sentimental half-dreams of Christmas, of sitting in my own home and lying in my own bed there, waiting with the warm magic that my father and mother were thoughtful enough to imbue me with. Though these remembrances came not without connection: while waiting with that warm magic there was also created a suspense and awaiting of fright, believing, back then *knowing*, that the jolly king of the North Pole was going to heave himself into the rooms downstairs in the coming silent hours.

About to fall fully asleep under these thoughts, and my tears, that night in the floating house, I heard a soft knock across the room from me. Not any sort of rapping knock knock, not a knock with human intent, but the gentle sound of something bobbing on a surface and grazing.

I was quite unable to move. I could neither gape across the taut vacuum the grownups had boxed me away in for the night, in a still bed in a still cosmos compacted into a single room, nor clothe myself in the covers and allow, without my seeing, whatever horror awaited to do whatever it darkly pleased.

Even my child's mind was full of things. Ghosts and grins and leaping white frames.

And floating people in a floating house.

The sound came of something brushed against wood.

On the other side of the room.

It came from far across the black that was relieved not by light, as none could make it through the thick patched curtains. I had been staring also at the lamp and the light fittings since I had been put to bed, and so my eyes had strained to a filtery grey. Black seeped out of the corners and tried to encircle whatever I saw. It tried to encircle the airing cupboard, from where I knew the noises came.

Up to my brims came terror such as I had not felt, and it seemed as though it might start surging out of my eye sockets. I felt as though I could not contain any of myself, and I had never needed to. I could not call mother here.

In the blackish grey I dared myself to do anything in the face of another brush. I did nothing and my skin, my flesh, felt very feeble and would not be able to hold in the stark fright now bulging inside of it. I could not call for the man and I could not turn on the light and I could not get down out of my bed and I could not leave the room into the dark outside where they would all be floating.

With my faculties strained beyond reason for an interminable period, there then came a sound of shifting, and I knew that the cupboard door had pushed open. I remember that I made a noise I had not been born to make.

The door did not creak as it might in known nightmares; instead it made a quiet and extended *whoosh*, as its bottom swept the carpet, and in the lack of light there was a lack of senses, a lack of sound save for the *whoosh* of the cupboard door, and then in the abhorrent smoky glaze of the night, I saw cramped in the cupboard and then very slowly cast out of it, for this all happened with the slow ache of unwanted time, the figure of a man untested by luminosity; he fell without gravity forwards till he rolled over in the midst of the air, during this unending surge towards my bed, and I was on the upper bed so the man was at my altitude, and my bladder and my bowels became suddenly full in a fit of movement echoed by the shaking of my hands and sheets. I believed nothing more in these moments than that I could not live through them.

I could just catch the aspects of the man's face as he tumbled and tapped the wall and bounced away from it towards the ceiling, and he looked very sullen and stretched and unwary as they all did, and as he twisted in slowest motion the brightest point in the room and in the galaxy became the measured whiteness of his eyes, which jittered about but never looked fully at me. The whites could not be whites in this dark, but focal greys that could not be gazed away from.

With a tap against the wall above the door, the man was given new orbit and came falling sideways towards my bed. I could not *not* move any longer with the knowledge that he lurched this way and I knew that I would surely die in some unknown manner. In fear, in brokenness, not bravery, I slithered shuddering off of the bed and bumped onto the floor, and moaning tugged the curtain which came loose in a heap, and I jumped up and pulled the latch, almost breaking it, and lifted the window as high and hard as I could, then lay on my back on the pile of blanket curtain and tried to remember how to breathe.

I lay there a long while, it seemed at least, with the floating man slowly bouncing and turning. The new sound of a thread of wind twining through the trees outside only amplified the silence of the room in which I was trapped, still, and the man was trapped, flying. My heart would have had me unconscious but my eyes would not.

A post of the bed twinged the man in his ghastly flight. It tipped him and the course changed. Over once so that he was upside down, and then shoulder first he went, with some knocks, floating right out of the window. He passed very closely by me in doing this, and so I leant hard into the floor and tried to become the curtains.

I saw, very closely, as I have mentioned: his FACE.

Then, I saw a leg of black trouser, and a foot, and the man was gone. I calmed for seconds before remembering the others in the house, though I was able later to stand, and look out, and to try to spot the man over the trees, in the garden, over the rooftops. The man was gone.

It was a relief until I knew that he had not gone nowhere, but somewhere.

The man who owned the house must have, at some point, heard either my jump out of the bed or the crash of the window opening, and taken a while then to come to, for he himself came crashing into the room eventually, straight to the window where he leant out of it, shouting, 'Oh NO!' before running downstairs, and I heard through the bedroom floor the door to the rear garden thrash in its hinges, and saw the man down in the garden looking up and about at the sky, searching for a surreal eclipse of stars in the shape of a person, something that should not ever be or be seen. Then after this looking, and there was nothing, the man squatted in the grass with his head in his hands, and I stood in the folds of blanket that had been stapled over the window, looking up at the sky which was not as full of stars or floating people as it was full of moon and clouds, and I have remembered this scene for the rest of my life, for the clouds were arranged in such a strange way that they looked like a riverbank.

An unheard phone call brought my father to the house, at an hour farthest from both dusk and dawn. The man had at some time stopped cowering in the garden and come inside, and he spoke very sternly and angrily at my father. He was not angry at my father, and I knew even then that he was very angry at me. My face was creased and I saw little through the tears.

The owner of the floating house said things but did not once look at me.

My father took me outside and put me distraught and exhausted into the car. I watched him smoke three cigarettes, which I counted, and then he leaned into the car to buckle my seatbelt, and then he climbed into the driver's seat and drove us away. I remember that he did not speak, and perhaps that he put on the radio.

I had been too young to question any of this and we did not speak of the floating house, and I did not return, ever again. It is a subject I dared not broach. When I was younger I remember some few glances thrown my way, a suggestion perhaps, that I had caught something I should not have seen. Then it went unmentioned even by my father's eyes.

I do wish I had not ever seen the floating house.

Especially I wish I had not seen the man who floated out of the airing cupboard.

I lie adrift in bed, wondering if there will be a knock at the window, and if I will turn to see, outside, some horrific body adrift, and eyes without fixing. Through fear of this I may well become very detached from everything, and float off of the floor myself.

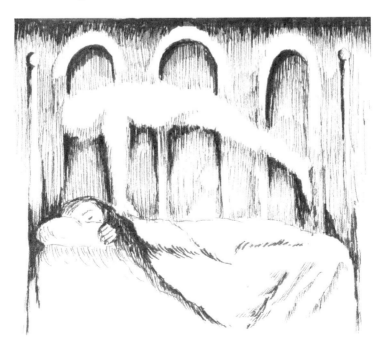

FEVER GIRLS

附

LINDA NIEHOFF

Fevers brought the dead and the girls knew it. In parlours they lay on rich red velvet couches that were used for swooning and loosening corsets. The girls watched as shadows of the dead danced on the walls.

They did everything they could to catch a fever. They walked the moonlit damp streets late alone. They stood under the flickering gaslight. They breathed in night air from the backs of houses. Late. After everyone went to bed they creeped down the talking stairs that moaned under each footstep, telling them not to go farther. They unclicked back doors beside still dinner-warmed kitchens. They put their faces through the cracks in the door and they breathed. In and in and in the cold death air that would bring a fever. That would bring the dead. They were a secret society. A club with a notebook and notes and meeting times.

It was Claire who fell in love.

Some said she got the name from the cemetery—that's the only way she could have known who the boy was. Claire and the others maintained it was the fevers. When the story was posted in all the papers, when strangers were knocking knocking knocking at her door she maintained all along that she had met the boy. They had fallen in love and were going to marry.

The fever had made her pale. Made her skin too white. Too bluish. Her eyes too large in her head. The other girls whispered behind their hands. She looked like a ghost bride.

Violet was terribly jealous, the most jealous of them all.

"Why does she get the boy when all I get are old Civil War soldiers or creepy little girls?"

Violet said in hushed tones to Maddy as they walked along under gray skies arm in arm. They had to whisper. The town was full of reporters by then. Newspapermen desperate for the story of the girls, the fevers, the dead.

Widows clutching lace handkerchiefs had knocked down their doors. Parents brought portraits of gloomy children, wanting to know if the society had seen them. What message did they bring? The mothers and widows and fiancées all wanted to know.

There was a rash of fevers after that. The hospitals were full. Everyone wanted to contact the dead. But all it ended up doing was making more dead. And so more fevers. And so more dead. And the girls became more famous. And Claire more famous still as she seemed not to be recovering at all.

Her picture was put in pulp stories. Put into the penny papers. Her eyes were dark and shadowed as she prepared, the printed words all said, for her wedding. Girls imitated her by staying out of the sun, taking ash from cold fireplaces and smearing it under their eyes. Coughing and swooning and walking in the night for love.

Some said she was really sick. Others said it was simply for show. Others that it was love that would bring symptoms like death. Only Claire knew. And she coughed too much to say for sure.

They shopped for gowns for her upcoming nuptials. No one was sure where the vows should be spoken or if she should wear black or white. Her father said his daughter would be married in the church. Her mother wondered should it be outside? In the graveyard? She wanted to be thoughtful and include the groom. And where would they live? She assumed the boy had no money, but selling the story had helped some. Her mother was secretly glad his parents were long dead so she wouldn't have to contend with another mother who wanted different things for the young couple.

Claire herself didn't say much on the matter. She spent nights with the window cracked, breathing in the moonlight hoping for another fever. It was hard to make arrangements without a fever. Without the boy. She was living only with the remembrance of his promise.

During the week they'd spent together, Claire had felt like a hot air balloon thin and translucent floating among the starlight, looking down on the blue shadows of all the people that were well. He had come as a flicker almost too beautiful to look at it. He'd promised so many things. So many things.

"It will always feel like this," he said. "Like dancing in starlight. Like floating. Like the translucent skin of a hot air balloon whisking us forever away."

His hair was like the sunlight on hay bales in late July fields. It was goblin blond and red all at once. His eyes were the color of moss. Would that be what it felt like? Always July? Always the time when the sun was falling just enough to make the world golden and reddish? Would it always feel like the silky moss in the stream that undulated in the cool cool water? Moving and flowing. The red of his hair. The moss-green of his eyes. She could smell summer on him. Claire thought that's what it would be like.

Sometimes the week with him had been like a flame that jumped too high, that threatened to break loose. Sometimes it was skin too hot to touch.

But ever since the fever, everything was gray and night blue. And her lungs still hurt to breathe, but she would crack her window while her parents made plans. Crack her window to breathe in another fever because she couldn't wait. Couldn't wait for the vows. She wanted the translucent and the heat and the stars and the red and the clear cold moss water now now now.

The newspapers found his grave. They drew the picture up in the paper, the fancy scrolls that lined his name. The unbloomed roses that stood forever waiting in clusters along the corners. Girls huddled around it longing for a glimpse of him. They dropped handkerchiefs with cursive initials hoping that in the night he would scratch their windows and take them up on deathly burning rides over the city the way he had with Claire. After all, they hadn't known that dead boys were in the market for marriage. This opened up whole new worlds.

The secret society was put on hold. Too many people—crying widows, newly childless parents, newspaper men—followed them when they went out, making it impossible to meet. Besides, Violet was still jealous. She wrapped her shawl around her shoulders and proclaimed that she wasn't in the business of nannying for the dead. What was the point of going forward if that was all she was wanted for?

Still she cried at her window when no one was watching and breathed and breathed and breathed the chilly night and hoped for something different.

The wedding day was set. Inside the church, they'd finally decided, with Claire in black. It was a compromise between her mother and father. And no one was sure how the groom would arrive. Violet hoped that he'd change his mind and then Claire would be there all alone in the front with all those people staring at her and all at once everyone including Claire would find out she was not so special after all.

Claire hadn't been able to reach him. Though her body had grown so thin and so frail, it still wouldn't produce a fever. She coughed and her whole body shook. She had to wheeze to get enough air. Some of the older married women said, "Surely he won't want her now. She's let herself go."

But Claire walked on her father's arm. Some said it was more like he was propping her up. They all strained to see if the boy was there.

was a flame that burned too high, too hot, that hurt to look at.

"We have a society, too," he said and smiled. Claire couldn't be sure if he even had any teeth at all.

At first, they thought she'd merely fainted, and later some said it was the pressure of being so famous just for love. Others said it was proof it had all been for show and those girls should have known it would come back to them—all that time in the night air.

In the end she collapsed before she could even whisper a word from her vows, and a week later, they lowered her into the ground. Her mother sobbed by the grave, "I thought they would live on earth." And, "I thought we'd see them both without the help of fevers."

The newspaper drew up pictures of the two of them—Claire with her wide eyes and black veil and the boy with light hay colored hair. "Together at Last," read the headlines. There were variations of this same theme for weeks. Two silhouettes walking through a graveyard, the tombstones their attendants. The lonely ones breathed at the night windows hoping for a glimpse of them. Until a movement rose up banning the society and any other such society. Death was too much in fashion. They said, "We'll be a city of dead if this doesn't stop." Women carried signs and demanded that their daughters be kept safe from dead boys like the one who came for Claire.

Others still secretly breathed in the chill night air, and Violet was among them. Why should Claire be the only one to live happily ever after?

Only Claire knew that he wasn't really a boy but something worse. And it didn't feel like floating. Not at all.

Would he float along in shadows on the wall? Would he suddenly pop up in the window?

Claire was covered by a black veil. Her wide eyes looked out among large lace roses. No one could tell if she worried or hoped. All of them looked at Claire and then looked all around the vaulted ceilings, trying to catch a glimpse of the boy with hair like fields in July. All of them wanted to see what a boy looked like who'd died too young but still held onto the earthly dream of love, of a girl, of a life together.

It was only Claire who saw him finally, and she cried out. It wasn't his hair that was red after all. It was his eyes. His hair was the color of mossy green, of one who's been in the grave too long. His eyes were the dying sun. His smile

Brigids Gate
PRESS
presents

Were Tales:
A Shapeshifter Anthology
Edited by S.D. Vassallo and Steven M. Long

Featuring Works By:

Cindy O'Quinn
S.H. Cooper
Shane Douglas Keene
Kev Harrison
Ruschelle Dillon
Baba Jide Low
Linda D. Addison
Alyson Faye
Catherine McCarthy
Tabatha Wood
Michelle Garza and
Melissa Lason
Eric J. Guignard
Beverley Lee

Cynthia Pelayo
Sara Tantlinger
Elle Turpitt
Stephanie Ellis
Theresa Derwin
Christina Sng
Clara Madrigano
Villimey Mist
H.R. Boldwood
Ben Monroe
Stephanie Wytovich
Laurel Hightower
Jonathan Maberry
Gabino Iglesias

Werewolves. Berserkers. Kisune. From the most ancient times, tales have
been told of people who transform into beasts. Sometimes, they're friendly and
helpful. Sometimes, they are tricksters. And sometimes they're terrifying.
Within the pages of "Were Tales," you will meet them all.

Available Now in Paperback and eBook

Camera's Eye

ঙ৪৩

Daniel David Froid

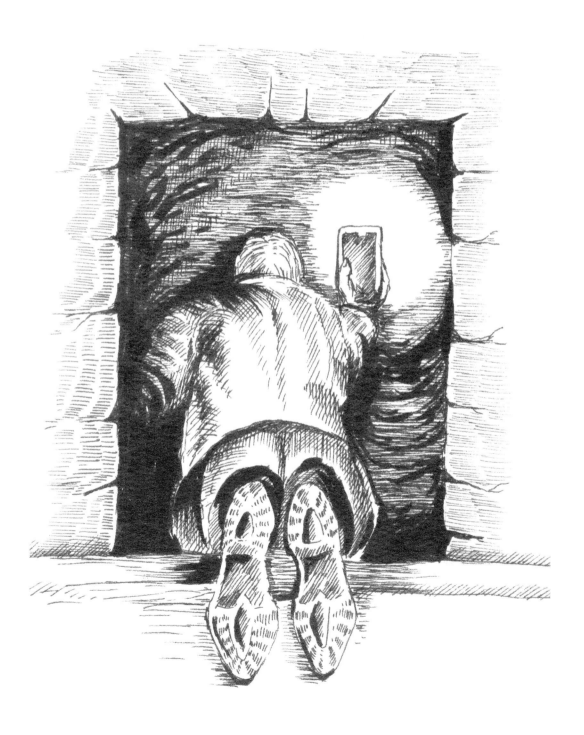

1.

All that's left now is the video.

Its quality is poor; the equipment, after all, had been heavily damaged throughout the process of recording. The camera was old, not digital, and heat exposure warped its plastic parts and ruined the film. It seems surprising, in fact, that it could record at all—or, rather, that the film could be retrieved and viewed afterward. The resulting video is foggy, and the colors are off. The saturation is all wrong.

The video is about four minutes in duration. As it opens, two people, a man and a woman, both of them sweaty and bedraggled and dressed in dirty clothes, slouch before the camera's eye. Another woman is recording, and her voice can be heard, but barely, as the camera pans over a dreary landscape. Everything looks the same. The parched clay beneath their feet, dry to the point of cracking, the lines forming honeycombs that go on and on; the yawning sky that seems somehow too low, as if the god of the morning had that day stumbled, bleary-eyed, and hung the firmament poorly— all is a sandy dirty grey-beige color, further washed out by the damage wrought by heat. At the edges of the frame, the film is streaked by lurid shades of pink. As the video proceeds, white splotches crackle here and there across the screen. Far in the distance, a speck of dark brown seems to suggest something else, a blot on the landscape, though it is hard to tell what it is: a city? Or perhaps it is only another defect in the film.

The trio might be in a lonely desert somewhere on earth, but they are, supposedly, in hell.

It is not so long ago, now, since the video's initial emergence, but it already seems like a myth: a story that never really happened but one that might still tell you a little bit of the truth. And this remains the case despite the brief flurry of reports, blogs, tweets, and sundry online chatter that once surrounded Angela and the others. Most thought of her as a crank and not much more. Can she be called a cult leader if her cult never really took off? But whatever anyone thinks of Angela, there remains the video, which even enthusiasts sometimes agree is, when it comes right down to it, a bit underwhelming within the entire apparatus of the mystery. Yes, its description, theoretical provenance, and very existence often seem far more tantalizing than the artifact itself. If this be hell, after all, one might hope for glimpses of its denizens, if not its leader, or of the torments deep in the pit—all those things of which we have always longed to know more. Instead, what we have is a heavily distorted glimpse of a vast bare desert and what is, apparently, a city in the background, along with the camerawoman's voice.

She sounds scratchy and wheezy; she sounds exhausted. Her voice cuts in and out. First she says something incomprehensibly garbled. She continues: "…standing on a…the ground and the sky"—the camera pans to show the honeycombed clay, the dead sky—"…is a city…and we now…center." The camera moves again, past the two tired travelers, slumped on the ground, and lingers for a moment on the brown speck that we guess is the aforementioned city, toward whose center they intended, perhaps, to go. Then the camera moves back to the travelers, and one of them, the man, gazes at the lens and mouths something inaudible. He looks like he has already died, he is so pale and worn out and haggard, yet the mouth on his grimacing face is moving. The other woman lies on the ground.

What happens next has become a source of debate and argument among those few who have become devoted to this peculiar artifact. At this point, the camera leaves the travelers behind, quickly, in a whirl of bleached-out beige, as if the camerawoman has been surprised by something offscreen. A whirl of movement, and some say that a creature—even a demon?—moves across the screen, surprising the trio, scaring the woman into dropping the camera. But most say that that is simply what they want to see: the video itself provides no evidence beyond an indistinguishable blur. There is only that whirl of movement, a splotch that might be a dark color or might be the effects of distortion, of the degradation of the film. Either way, at this point the video ends.

This is the recording that evidently made its way back to our world, lodged in the camera carried in the arms of the soon-dead cinematographer, Judith, who had just barely returned from the devil's domain. She averred that that was where she was going. Swore, that is, in a letter found in a certain house in whose basement her corpse was discovered, the camera strapped to her chest. In the basement of this house in Wallace, Nebraska, there had once, it seems, been a certain doorway, and Judith had accompanied two of her friends or associates inside, and, after a very long journey, they made it to this vast infernal desert where she pulled out her camera and recorded some footage, and then—

And then her body was discovered in the basement of her home. It was Angela, her sister, who discovered the body, and it was she who called the police, and most agree that it was she who orchestrated everything that followed. Everything: her sister's funeral, the attempted sale of the house, its eventual demolition. She likewise set in motion the initial report in the Wallace newspaper, the *Daily*; published the video online (and took it down, and put it up again); drummed up a veritable storm of publicity that died faster than she wished, though she soon disappeared, and nobody knows what became of her or why she worked so hard for such a short time at publicizing the video, only to vanish herself.

The video continues to pop up online now and then, but it almost never stays for long. Or, if the video remains, then interest resembles the lives of the mayflies: an intense buzz, a swarm that fades and dies within a day. Yes, she, and it, continue to hold some interest for certain enthusiasts of obscure and faded delusions, who congregate on dead-end blogs, unfashion-able forums where updates are slow but certain, eventually, to come; social media posts, which are recirculated, or at least dug up and admired, here and there. The interviews Angela did are hard to find now, both articles and videos, though certainly some might have tucked them away somewhere on their hard drives or somewhere in an invisible cloud. That the group had vanished; that the mysterious deaths of the people visible in the video seemed to be connected; that the video exists at all add to the aura of mystery about which most simply did not care in the end, but about which some cared very much for a very brief period of time.

Angela's fame is, then, but a tiny footnote in the history of conspiracy. Her story belongs to a curious tribe, but one which will always have its gawkers and adherents. The others, her associates, those featured in the film, their names are hardly mentioned, if anyone still knows them at all. When the film once again makes the rounds, shared by a new batch of the curious and the naïve, some of them smirk and roll their eyes; some of them stop and watch and frown, thinking, "That's it?" Some claim as well that the video is surely a fraud. Those who feature in the video could simply be standing on, say, the fractured earth of the California desert; they could be hired actors or enthusiastic amateurs. But true believers have their reasons. *Look at the sky*, they might say: *the sky on earth has never looked like that. Look how dead it is, how low.* Or they cite the weight of evidence, however dubious, in the forms of obituaries, news reports, and so on, much of which could certainly be traced back to Angela. But belief remains, always, far preferable to doubt.

Yes, this group always finds its members, or, rather, its members always seek and find others of their kind. Watching the video, these select few feel a dark and pleasurable shiver, a thrum somewhere low in the belly, which feels a little like longing and a little like fear. They thrill at the mystery, and they will, as is the habit of their kind, begin to ferret out whatever pieces of the puzzle they can find. They will find like-minded others in whom they will feel that thrill or thrum mirrored back to them, who will share it. These few feel—and they are correct—that they have glimpsed a secret, something dredged up from the bottom of the world. It is this private intensity they are after. It is like inhaling some heady, sweet, and rich fume, such as gasoline. It changes them because they allow it to do so and because they want it to do so.

2.

Inhaling the fume, letting it wash over him, he watched the video many, many times, which led him to the blogs, which led him to the others, which led him to what he is now doing. He has come to the house where Judith died. However he did it—scouring records online, spending hours on the phone with tired and bleak office clerks who did not wish to speak to him, who knows—he rooted out her address. He wanted to see it, to see what he could find. Once he had ascertained the house's location and outlined a plan, he settled on a date and drove down to Wallace to carry it out.

Upon arrival, perhaps he found Wallace small and dreary, its streets lined with dilapidated buildings in need of a power wash or, better yet, of demolition. Perhaps he was put off by this dire place, or perhaps he thought it looked just right for what it was, the backdrop to the saga of Angela and Judith. Wallace was not far from his own home, ninety miles away, though he remarked before leaving that he had never before been there.

He would have parked downtown, such as it is—a few close blocks of poorly kept brick buildings—in front of a diner, say, or the Goodwill, or the public library, and stepped out of his car, wearing a nondescript outfit: faded blue jeans and a button-up shirt in green plaid or something like. Though those few he must have passed on the sidewalk would have glanced his way, their faces surely did not show suspicion or distrust. But why would they? This town was not so small that they would be shocked at the arrival of a stranger. Still, he would have felt on edge, which cast shadows on everything and everyone he saw, and it would have been his face, not theirs, that betrayed suspicion.

From his car, he would have moved swiftly toward his destination, having studied maps sufficiently to memorize his route and to make his movement look natural. He would not have nervously glanced at his phone, pulled up the route, conspicuously followed it. No. He would have been more careful. If he parked on the main through-street downtown, Sherman Avenue, he would have gone four blocks north, then left, three blocks down 12th Street, then right. He would have walked swiftly but not too fast—a natural pace—and tried to move confidently down the street, as if he were a man who knew where he was going. But he was; he was going to Judith's.

He would have passed rows of rundown houses, children playing in the front yard, their parents sometimes glancing at him from the stoop. The buildings he passed, as well as their residents, must have seemed to him then as sun-bleached and damaged, as unknowable as the scenes and the people in the video.

Judith's house sits in the middle of Birch Street, closely flanked by similar-looking houses on either side. The yards on this street are narrow and negligible patches of thirsty brown grass. From outside, Judith's house is truly nothing special: ranch-style, pale yellow siding, its low-pitched roof gabled in a dull earthy brown. Anyone can, as he did—if they know the address—pull it up on an online map; anyone can see it for themselves. Knowing that nobody lived here or had done for years, he would no doubt have been self-conscious about his approach. The neighbors, if they were home, may well have wondered what it was that a stranger was doing there at a house they themselves may have feared or regarded as an anomalous blight.

And so he would have moved past the house, not lingering too much in the front, and taken a left at the end of the block. His close study of a satellite view of the area would have informed him that an alley stretched behind the houses here, a narrow wedge of unkempt grass between identical, blank backyards. It would have made sense for him to turn down the alley and, in that way, reach the back of the house. No fence barred him from approaching, but when he reached the back door he surely would have discovered that it was locked. Who has the keys, he may have wondered then: perhaps Angela, wherever she is now. That there was no evidence of intruders, of any previous attempts at break-ins, probably pleased him. He wanted to experience a first, to see something no one else had seen—at least, no one who was not involved firsthand. He wanted likewise to avoid any trouble.

The house was old and unoccupied and, therefore, free of updated fixtures and windows. It seems conceivable, then, that he might have moved to the right of the back door, approaching a sash window. It was probably then that he took a pair of gloves out of one pocket and put them on. Perhaps he put the gloves on as soon as he reached the backyard, so that no fingerprints would have shown on the doorknob. But did he care about that?

Anyway, it would have seemed a fairly simple matter to him to pull a screwdriver from his back pocket, slide it beneath the glass, and wiggle it around, attempting to loosen the glass in its frame. But here, perhaps, emerged a moment of drama: the pressure of the screwdriver as it twisted back and forth may have caused the old glass to crack, and then to loosen, and, finally, to shatter. It could have happened that way. If so, then it is possible that he swore, hopped backward, and looked around him, shaken, for observers. The nerves must have been getting to him, now, if not before. Still, his arrival during the day had been intentional: he weighed the exposure of broad daylight against the possibility that most of the neighbors would be at work.

Once he had assured himself that nobody had noticed him, he would have reached his hand into the frame, maneuvering it around the glass, unlocking the window, and carefully inching it upward. At last, having pulled his hand out, he would have pushed the frame up with both hands. The gloves had been a good idea after all. He probably felt quite clever.

Pulling himself inside, he looked around. Where would the window have opened—in a back room, once a bedroom or an office? Whatever it used to be, whatever used to happen there, the room now was empty, free of furniture and decorations: no signs of what it once contained, the function it once performed. Perhaps the door opened into a hallway with more bare rooms, all shut. Probably he scoped each of them out, one by one, finding, who knows, more bedrooms, a bathroom, closets. It was only when he reached the end of the hall that he stopped, in a large open room with a beaten-up chesterfield and a rickety end table: the living room.

At this point, he pulled out his phone—removing the glove and then putting it back on when he was done—and tapped and rubbed the glass until he accessed the correct application. He tapped the red button that began the recording. At last. We've been waiting for this. We watch.

3.

The video begins.

"Here we are," he says. He moves past this open room, searching for the door to the basement. "Living room," he announces. "Kitchen." He walks into the latter room, moving the camera around in the dim light, showing off once-white cupboards, dusty counters. He walks in and looks around, and the camera moves with his body. Finally he reaches the kitchen's back corner, pulls the door toward him, and walks down the steps. From out of the stairwell, he emerges into the basement. "The basement," he says. "Here we are," he repeats. He's a little awkward, his voice eager and high-pitched and boyish. He fumbles for a light switch and finds one. The switch turns on a harsh fluorescent light, which casts the startlingly bright and clean white Berber carpet, the stark white walls, in its unpleasant glow.

In the basement, he finds himself facing a choice. On his left is the half of the basement that is finished, and the camera reveals a few paintings, which seem to depict nature scenes—though it is hard to tell, at least for us—that still hang on the walls, along with an armchair and an empty bookcase. On his right is a doorway covered by a thin black curtain. He moves right, entering the half of the basement that is not finished, a warren of rooms whose walls and floor are both simple poured concrete and whose ceiling beams are exposed. Seeing nothing of interest at first, he moves through the rooms swiftly, camera darting around along with him as he searches for, we suppose, clues. What does a doorway to hell look like? How will he, or we, know it when it comes into view?

The first unfinished room is utterly empty. There is nothing here whatsoever. The poor lighting in this room—only the fluorescent light glows behind him—seems to distort the concrete walls and floor. As they are all the same color and texture, and curiously shadowed, it is difficult to tell where the floor ends and the walls begin. He moves on. In the next room, the camera shows us the HVAC unit, against a wall whose beams are exposed, like the ceiling in the previous room. Next to the unit is a stack of cardboard boxes. He moves closer. He must be peering at them; the camera lingers, and blooms of mold are visible on the boxes' upper flaps. But he doesn't touch them; he moves on. Here he has to reach out a hand and slide a paneled wooden door into a recess in the wall.

It is impossible not to feel, at this point, a shiver of dread. That he is getting closer to *it* feels palpable, unmistakable. A feeling of trepidation that is very much like desire begins to take root within us. We can tell he feels it too. His breathing grows heavier from behind the camera's eye. Whatever he finds back there, he, and we, will be the first to see it. We hope the signal lasts, the signal that allows us to follow him here.

The next room is very small, and in it we find a large utility sink or tub. It stands on metal legs, and it is covered in brown rust. Next to it is a toilet, its lid closed. The camera briefly flashes over both and moves away. Near the toilet is a small door. Now he faces the door that conceals the crawlspace beneath the stairs down which he just walked. The far wall, the one perpendicular to the door, is scarcely a wall at all; it ends three-fourths of the way to the ceiling, where behind it a hole exposes part of the house's foundations, set into the earth. He says, somewhat unhelpfully, "I can see underneath the house."

He has now described the circumference of a circle; he has twirled about the room and glances at the path he has just taken. The camera does, too.

This room must reek. As if he has read our thoughts, he says, "It's damp. I can smell it." He must feel a flush of pleasure at having arrived here. We wonder if he felt drawn to this corner; somehow it just seems right. He must have known he would reach this corner and would know what to do next. He knew the others, us, were waiting for him, and that we are watching. Perhaps the signal will not last for very much longer, but he is foolish enough to try, and we are eager to watch him try.

All of us united by our mutual pleasure—all of us breathing in syncopation, waiting for the unbearable moment we need, when he opens the door—we continue to watch. He moves toward the hole. He peers into the house's foundations, surely straining to see if what he wants is in here. But it isn't, he knows; it's just tightly packed earth and beams of wood. He knows that what he wants lies behind the door beside him, inside the crawlspace. He allows the camera to linger, lovingly, on the battered old door. Its white paint is chipped. Spiders' cobwebs have piled up in the corners.

And now he flings out a hand and opens the door, which reveals a set of stairs to a second basement below. His breathing still so heavy, but sounding somehow muffled, somehow soft, he moves down the steps. Then he stops, rubbing the glass on his phone until a flashlight flickers on: now we can all of us see.

The stairs are made of wood. He whispers, "They feel soft." He treads down the stairs, and we see a cockroach scurry across the floor. It is made of concrete, even rougher, older-looking, than the floor above. The room looks small: probably, he cannot even stand to his full height. The camera surveys the room, and we see a little warren in the corner—a tunnel. We do not even know if the tunnel, much less the room, is physically possible. We think back: when we went down the stairs, did we see the underside of the other stairs above him? We do not think we did. We are watching and wondering where we are. He approaches the tunnel, which is no more than three feet high, perhaps less. He crawls in, his phone leading the way. Is it possible that, in this way, we are even closer to whatever it is than he? We feel so close. We are breathing in and out, each of us together but separate, measuring the intake of oxygen carefully. We are peering into this impossible place—is this the bottom of the world, from where the secret will be dredged up?—and it feels like time has stopped. We are caught in this moment with him. He moves deeper and deeper. His phone bobs up and down as he crawls on knees and one hand. He breathes and grunts. He says, in a low voice that jolts us—it seems so loud— "It's hot in here."

After a time, a light gives off a glow in the distance. Some of us swear there is a shimmer, a light. We are breathless now.

Perhaps he thinks of us then, in this moment. Perhaps he wonders what we are thinking.

What some of us are thinking as we watch is that this cannot last for long. The signal will fade, the livestream will die, and we will be left in suspense. He should have recorded a video and uploaded it later. But the stunt proved too irresistible. And, besides, are we not rapt, overcome by the most exquisite terror?

Moving on, he continues to breathe and grunt.

But then something happens. A splotch of color, which might be a darkish red, which might be the color of the skin of an unknown creature, flies across the screen. The camera is rapidly moving, as though the phone has been slapped from his hand. He screams. It is more like a yelp, a pathetic little noise.

The video ends.

We gasp. Some of us scream. We swear and ask ourselves what happened. Then we ask each other. We try to rewind, slow it down, review what it is that we saw. But all we can see is the same blur of color that shifts and causes the phone that houses the camera to fly into the air. Fade to black. It's over. But we know for certain what proves to be true: he is gone, and we will never hear from him again, and, if anyone travels to Judith's house—the police or a curious adherent—they will likely not find him. Or they will find no more than a corpse, like Judith's.

Still, he has left something for us, over which we will pore. Even as we cannot help but ask ourselves what happened, even as we quietly mourn him, he has left us with something we will cherish and for which we fervently thank him. All that's left now is the video.

JOURNEY INTO THE OCCULT,
WHERE HISTORY IS HORROR

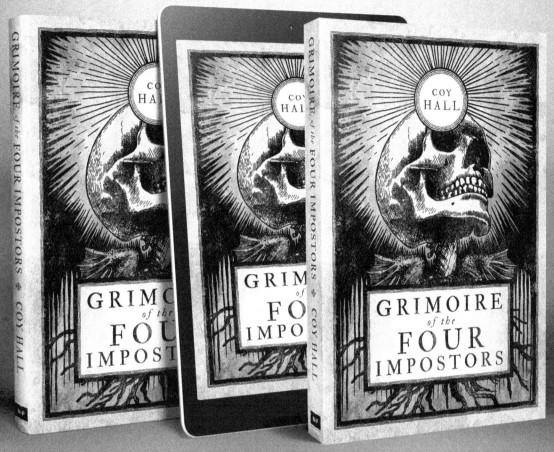

"…a banquet of words and haunting imagery, that takes a reader by the hand and leads them through tantalising and horrific tales. The writing is sublime, both ancient in feel but very understandable, and the richness of the characters leaps off the page. There are genuine disturbing moments, the kind of dread that settles softly and you find yourself thinking about afterwards; the kind that buries deep…there are dark, compelling delights at work here. One of my favourite reads of 2021!"
—Beverley Lee, author, Goodreads review

ARACHNIDS IN YOUR BED:

AN INTERACTIVE BEDTIME STORY FOR CHILDREN— AND ADULTS

CR&O

SARINA DORIE

In the morning, you wake up. As you cram your feet into your _____, (Choose one: *slippers/shoes/shoes without socks/cement shoes*) something moves. It was probably a spider. Don't worry, most are not poisonous.

○

On your way to _____, (Choose one: *school/work/the unemployment office/take over the world*) something falls from the _____, (Choose one: *bus/automobile/ sky/submarine*) onto your head. Was it a spider?

Most likely.

○

Fun Fact: Some species of ants are attracted to electronics.

Do you know what eats ants? You guessed it—Spiders!

What do you think is hanging out behind your computer?
A. Ants
B. A spider
C. A dead rat
D. Ants covering a dead rat, with spiders living inside, about to burst out at any moment.

○

As you sit at your desk, something tickles your ankle. You look down. Did you just see a spider?

Maybe it was a _____. (Choose one: *dust bunny/scorpion/zombie/Republican*)

○

Unsurprisingly, your ankle itches. It is swollen and lumpy. What did this to you? Is this an allergic reaction?

No, these are bites from a spider.

If you could only select one to make you feel better, which would you choose?
A. Benadryl
B. Hydrocortisone
C. Bug spray
D. An ax

In case you're wondering, it doesn't matter what you choose. You don't have any of these.

○

Fun Activity: Protect yourself with a barrier of bug spray by circling all the spiders you see.

* *
* *

No, those are not asterisks. Those are spiders.

Some of their legs got bit off. By each other.

Did you circle all of them? I think you missed some, and they got away.

○

There is a tickle on the back of your neck. It's just a tag in your clothes, you say. Most definitely not a spider.

Only, you don't have a tag in your shirt. Maybe you should check. That is your interactive activity for this section.

○

It's time to put your hand in some dark places full of spider webs. Which is the safest?

A. The back of the closet.
B. Under the bed.
C. Behind the guillotine gathering dust in the corner.
D. All of the above are perfectly safe.

Do you know the correct answer? That's right. None of the above.

Didn't see that option? That's because you have to stick your hand in all those places today. Lucky you!

○

Fun Activity: Can you find three spiders in this room? No?

Look harder. They can find you.

○

Fun Fact: Female spiders like to make a home in dark tunnels and caverns.

Noses are hollow tunnels that lead to the sinus cavity, which is basically a cavern.

Why do furry brown body parts fill your snot when you blow your nose? I think you know why.

Fun Activity: After you blow your nose, count how many legs you find in your tissue.

○

It's time to get in bed. You throw back your covers. Something dark and furry quickly escapes under the blankets. Is your bed partner a spider?

Maybe it was a _____, (Choose one: snake/sasquatch/bear/Democrat).

On the other hand, it might have only been a spider.

○

Is that a shadow on the ceiling? Did it just move? Could it be something that rhymes with "wider?"

If you said "woolly mammoth," you are incorrect.

○

What's that tickle in your ear?

A. A poisonous spider. Obviously.
B. A hair. Even though you have felt for hairs, made sure no hairs are near your ear, you shaved your head, and now are bald. It has to be a hair, not a spider.
C. The leg of a black widow spider in your ear canal. It is trying to exit, but can't because it crawled inside when it was small, and it is now too large to escape.
D. A fly caught in the spider's web that is frantically thrashing around as it tries to escape.
E. All of the above. Duh.

I think you know the correct answer to this.

○

Did something just brush against your arm? How well do you know the terrain of your bed? Did you catch the little guy earlier that escaped?

Activity Time: Look under all the pillows, shake out the blankets, and check for furry friends.

I'm not talking about a sasquatch.

Fun Fact: Did you know spiders molt and shed their exoskeleton?

That spider that you crushed earlier might not have been a spider. It might have been a husk that had been shed.

The real spider is watching from the corner. Waiting.

Spiders are attracted to moisture. Your mouth is moist. You remember to keep your mouth closed... until you fall asleep.

What caused you to wake up choking?

(Hint: You hope it wasn't a _____. (Choose one: *velociraptor/horse's head/ black hole sucking all air from the room/fermenting rat covered in ants with spiders about to burst out*).

Good night. Sleep tight. Don't let the arachnids bite. Not that you have a choice. We will do as we please, human.

Coming Soon! Four more delightful bedtime stories guaranteed to awaken your phobias and keep you up at night:

Dead Rats in the Back of Your Oven
Bears in Your Closet
An Octopus Behind Your Desk
The Fascist Neo-Nazis Under Your Bed

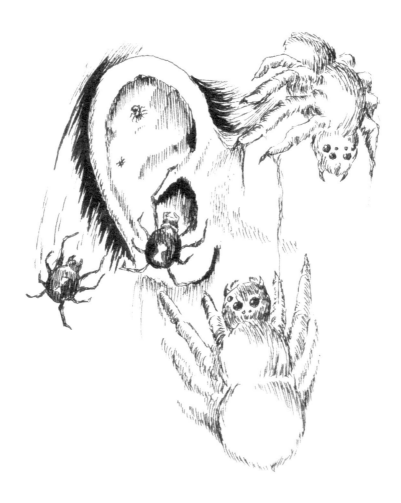

Milk Teeth

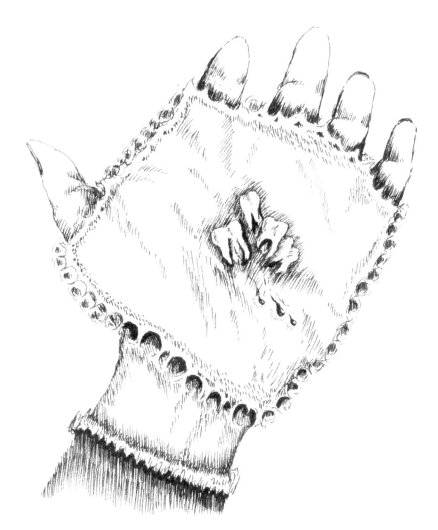

Annika Barranti Klein

The first time Father went away was the week of my twelfth birthday. He left without warning and was gone for three days. It was before Grandmother's palsy, before I met Jeet, before the teeth and so many other things. It was even before the wolves.

"Erzsébet," Father told me before he left, "you are not a woman yet, but you will be soon. So you must put away childish things."

I did not know what Father meant by childish things. Was it childish to read books? To sit in my window seat, watching across the meadow and waiting for something to happen? To sit in the parlor by the fire, knitting seemingly endless yards and yards of lace for my hope chest? I did not know.

After Father left, while it was still light out, Grandmother took me to the mirror on the landing and asked me to show her my teeth. I did, and she clucked and nodded and said nothing more.

The wolves came that night. Grandmother asked me to draw the curtains, and I saw them sitting on their haunches, looking at the house. I went from window to window, drawing the curtains as Grandmother asked, and looking out at the wolves. They were sitting in a ring around the entire house, shoulder to shoulder. They were inside the fence, only yards from the house. Grandmother did not say a word about them, only had me draw the curtains.

The next day Grandmother showed me a new knitting stitch pattern and kept me busy at my lace all day. I suppose, then, that knitting is not a childish thing. That night the wolves came again. I do not know how many wolves there were. Dozens. Perhaps hundreds. One huge wolf, much larger than all the others, walked the circle, weaving among the seated wolves.

The third day and night were the same.

On the fourth day, Father came back. The wolves did not come that night. "Not yet," Grandmother told him.

Father did not speak again of putting away childish things. Father rarely tells me anything twice. He brought me a book when he returned, so at least I knew that reading was not a childish thing to his eyes. I put the book under my pillow and slept with it there for one moon cycle.

○

Father went away again the next month.

Grandmother once again had me draw the curtains every night.

I hurt my finger and could not knit lace, so I sat in my window seat looking out over the meadow and read the book Father had brought me. It was a tale of terror, about a man who transformed into a monster called Mr. Hyde.

Something about it got under my skin; I could feel the terror of it in my ribs, pulling at me, whispering to me. Something was at once familiar and repulsive about it. I read for two days.

On the third day, I put the book in the stove.

I spent the rest of the day looking out over the meadow, no knitting or book in hand. That night when I went to bed, I felt something under my head. I lifted my pillow and found the charred remains of the book. I stuffed my fist into my mouth to keep from screaming, though there was no one to hear me if I did. Grandmother is old and hard of hearing, and besides she sleeps in the tower, on the other side of many empty rooms.

○

The next day when Father returned he remarked on the shadows below my eyes. I had slept not a wink all night, terrified as I was of the book he'd given me. I could not tell him.

"You should be walking," Father told me. "A girl needs fresh air."

So I took up walking, mornings after porridge and afternoons before tea.

I walked the fences that ringed our property. I suppose we were rich. The fences were long, and well-kept. I could not see how the wolves got in, unless they jumped over. I could not understand why the wolves only came when Father was away.

○

Father went away again. Grandmother had me draw the curtains again. I hated to do it. Twilight was my favorite time of day. With the curtains drawn it was as though the moon never rose in her full glory, only waxed to her most gibbous and protuberant point before disappearing for three days and reappearing, still gibbous but turned about and ready to wane again.

The moon was like a lady dressing behind a screen, only I never got to see her in her gown.

I took my walk that morning, staying closer to the house. I was worried about Grandmother. She did not seem like herself. When I returned home, I found her in her tower, seated on the settee, reading. I sat next to her and she handed me her book. It was her favorite, *Jane Eyre*. I read her favorite passages aloud, and when she fell asleep for her nap I sneaked out of her room and went for my afternoon walk. I was careful to be home before dark, but found myself walking faster for the last quarter mile, as I heard animals in the woods. I was steps from the front path when I heard a howl. I turned around and saw a giant wolf inside the fence, rushing at me.

I ran up the path to the front door and fumbled with the catch. The wolf was nearly upon me when I wrenched the door open, flung myself through, and slammed it shut.

In the morning, Grandmother was unwell. Half of her face was unmoving, and she could not speak to me. I did not know what to do. I climbed up onto her bed with her and clung to her like a child, afraid and uncertain. She had wet herself and the bed was soaked through, but Grandmother could not get up and besides, I could not lift the mattress.

At noon there came a knocking at the door. A great pounding that shook me awake, terrified at first, then grateful because it meant help had come. I threw on my dressing gown and rushed down the stairs.

I opened the door and found a strange man on the step, examining the doorframe where two large scratches cut deep into the wood. Scratches that had not been there before. I saw, too, a clump of fur caught in the latch. He had not noticed. I put my hand over it.

"Are you the lady of the house?" he asked, and I laughed at the absurdity. I was only a child, and it seemed that I would never be a lady.

"My name is Erzsébet. My grandmother is the lady of the house."

"Is she at home? I need—but where are my manners? My name is Stuart Greenwood. Doctor Stuart Greenwood. I am on my way to Oxborough and my carriage wheel has broken near your gate. I had hoped to find assistance here. Do you have a handyman, or stable man,

who might help me?"

"You're a doctor?" I repeated, dumbfounded at my luck.

"Yes. I am expected in Oxborough. I'll be taking over Dr. Briar's practice."

"My grandmother is sick. Can you help her? We do not have a groundskeeper but I can walk with you to the neighbors' house. They keep a full staff."

"What seems to be wrong with your grandmother, Erzsébet?"

"I don't know. She cannot get out of bed and doesn't speak." I began to cry and wished that I could stop myself. I felt like such a child just then, helpless and frightened.

Dr. Greenwood turned away from me and my stomach felt hard. He turned back just as quickly. "I'm going to my carriage for my bag. Will you put a kettle on?"

I ran to the fire and stoked it, then filled the kettle. I was hungry suddenly, but would not allow myself to eat until Dr. Greenwood had examined Grandmother.

It seemed to take a long time for him to come back with his bag. I began to think he would not return, and then suddenly he was in the hall, calling to me.

"Erzsébet?" he said, so informal—but then, he did not know our family name. He could not. It has been a long time since everyone in the countryside knew the name that went with the crest over our door.

"Yes!" I called back, anxious to have been away from Grandmother for so long.

Dr. Greenwood came up the stairs behind me, matching my hurried pace. He started at the mirror on the landing, but kept going after the briefest of hesitation. I ran down the hall and up the steps to Grandmother's room, the doctor following several paces behind. She stirred, more than she had moved yet that day, and made a sound. She didn't speak, but I knew she was trying to.

Dr. Greenwood came straight past me as I dallied several paces from the bed. He walked to Grandmother's side and spoke softly to her.

"My name is Dr. Greenwood. I'm here to help you. Can you take my hand? Good. Can you squeeze? Good. Now let's try the other hand."

He was gentle and patient with Grandmother, who could do none of what he asked, but followed him with one eye, the other drooping half shut.

He turned to me.

"What is your grandmother's name? Her given name?"

"Mrs. Ethelynne Penderghast," I told him, trying to rise to my full height to make him understand: Grandmother was a lady.

He showed a flicker of recognition, but then it was gone and he smiled. "Did you put that kettle on?"

"Yes," I told him. Of course I had. He'd asked me to, hadn't he?

"Good. Will you make us tea? Plenty of sugar for your grandmother, and good rich cream if you have any."

We did not keep cows, but there was a bottle of milk left in the ice box. I carefully removed the wire from the top and pulled out the stopper, then dug the cream out with the back end of a spoon. I put it in a teacup for Grandmother, measured the tea into the teapot, and poured hot water from the kettle. Then I arranged the teapot, cups and saucers, the milk bottle, and the sugar bowl on a tray and carried it up the stairs. I glanced at myself in the mirror on the landing and I looked very small.

Dr. Greenwood stayed with us all afternoon. We drank our tea and fed Grandmother spoonfuls of hers. He helped me to move Grandmother to her chair, and I cleaned her up while he hefted the mattress off the bed, carrying it downstairs and outside, where he said the sun would make it good as new tomorrow; Father could carry it back up when he returned. He made a new bed for Grandmother on her settee, and I opened her chest of drawers in search of linens.

Grandmother had a drawer full of teeth.

I slammed the drawer shut and opened the one below it. It held handkerchiefs and under-garments. Then I remembered Grandmother's trunk, a great brass-knuckled thing with a curved lid. The brass trimmings were oxidized to near-black, and the key was not in the lock. I went to Grandmother, dozing in her chair, and gently lifted the great brass locket she wore always around her neck. I opened it and the key was inside, between the likenesses of her mother and grandmother.

I knelt before Grandmother's trunk. I had never been allowed to open it, but I needed linens for her settee. The key turned smoothly in the lock and I lifted the heavy lid. Inside the trunk I found wool blankets and clean linens. I carried them to the settee and went back to close the trunk. Inside it, at the bottom, were what appeared to be old linens, stained a rusty brown and shredded. I shut the lid.

Dr. Greenwood and I made up Grandmother's new bed, with wool below the linens as well as above. Grandmother could not use a bedpan and I could not lift her. Dr. Greenwood carried her to the settee and made her comfortable.

"When does your father return?" he asked, and I realized for the first time that I was alone with a strange grown man.

"Tomorrow," I told him truthfully.

Would he expect payment for his services? I knew where father kept a purse, and could give him money. But perhaps he would not want money. I remembered suddenly that I was in my dressing gown, and looked down at myself. I was plump and round but not yet womanly.

Dr. Greenwood looked down at me and smiled.

"You poor child. You must be hungry. I have kept you working all day."

"No, sir. I mean, yes, sir, I am hungry, but I have been rude in neglecting to offer you dinner. May I prepare a meal for you?"

He protested, but I had cold chicken pie and we ate it in the drawing room in front of the fireplace, where I built a fire.

"I promised to walk you to the neighbor, but the sun is setting and there are wolves. Will you stay the night in father's room?"

He started at the mention of wolves.

"What did you say your father's name is?"

"Trnka."

He seemed to relax on hearing Father's name. It is not the name that goes with the family crest. That name belongs to Grandmother, and was my mother's name, too. Dr. Greenwood settled into Father's room.

That night I did not draw the curtains, and the wolves came up to the house, whining at the windows. I sat in my window seat until midnight, looking through the glass at them.

When I went upstairs, I took my pillow and blankets and slept on Grandmother's floor.

○

Father returned. He paid Dr. Greenwood handsomely, though Dr. Greenwood protested. Father made sure Dr. Greenwood's carriage wheel was repaired, then sent for a nurse from the city. Grandmother improved some, and Father moved her from the tower to the room near the kitchen, so that she could get around using the chair the nurse brought her. It was a high-backed wicker chair with large wheels that glided smoothly across our stone floors. She regained enough strength in her arm to propel herself, but couldn't get far with only one good arm, so I pushed her where she needed to go. She would grunt and gesture and we got to where we understood each other again.

When the month drew to a close and the moon was nearly full, I heard Father talking to Grandmother.

"I can't leave you," he told her, "not like this."

Grandmother looked angry and sad and she spoke as clearly as she had since the palsy struck: "You must."

○

So Father went away again just as the moon reached fullness, bringing Grandmother's nurse back to the city with him. I watched the two men leave, Father tall and broad and the nurse tall and narrow.

That night I started to draw the curtains and Grandmother became distressed. I went to her and she took my hands and spoke. I could not understand her words, but I thought I understood her meaning.

"You want me to leave them open?" I asked. She nodded, her head lolling to one side.

I wheeled her over to the window overlooking the meadow and took up my spot on the window seat. The sun set, the moon rose, and the wolves came. The large wolf whined at the window again, and Grandmother leaned over the arm of her chair and placed her palm against the glass. The wolf leaned his head against her hand, separated by the glass. I watched in horror and fascination.

Eventually Grandmother fell asleep and I righted her in her chair, wheeling her close to the dying fire. I slept on the rug that night.

I woke in the wee hours when the fire had died down and the moonlight was shining in through the window. The house was very still. I put a log on the embers in the fireplace, then crept to the window and peered out. The wolves were sitting in their circle, looking at the house; unmoving.

Grandmother called out in her sleep then: "Robert?" I did not know who Robert was. My mother's name was Robina, which is the feminine of Robert, but I did not know a Robert. I drew the curtains, tucked Grandmother's blanket around her, and settled myself back in front of the fire.

Grandmother woke in good spirits. I made us breakfast and wheeled Grandmother out into the kitchen garden, where we drank tea—I had taken to making it more frequently on Dr. Greenwood's recommendation, in order to get the good rich cream into her, since she could not eat much. Her arm was strong enough to hold the teacup herself, and she sat happily in the garden, saucer in her lap, babbling about nothing. Or so I thought. After a time I thought I heard her say "wolf," and I asked her to say it again, but she smiled and was quiet.

That night I tried again to draw the curtains and again she protested. Again she sat near the window. Again she reached out and touched the wolf through the glass. This time I felt more fascination than revulsion. I fell asleep on the window seat.

In the morning I woke to find myself still on the window seat, covered by a warm blanket. I stood and looked around; I was alone. The house was cold and I wrapped myself in the blanket before going to look for Grandmother.

I found her asleep in her chair in the garden, with the grasses around her trodden and broken. There was strange fur in her lap.

"Grandmother? Have you been out here all night?"

She nodded and grinned at me.

She would not say a word about her night in the garden with the wolves, no matter how much I pleaded with her to tell me what had happened.

That night I wheeled her to her room, drew all of the curtains, and locked all of the doors. I slept on the kitchen floor, listening for her, but no sounds woke me.

When Father returned, he did not bring back Grandmother's nurse. I did not know how to tell him what had happened, so I said nothing. Grandmother grew stronger so quickly that I half thought the night outside had cured her. It rained for three days and I grew restless and irritable. Finally it was dry.

I began taking my walks again.

It was autumn and the leaves were turning colors. The birch trees were yellow, the maples red and the elms orange. The grasses were still green, thanks to the rain. I walked the fence, trying not to think about how the wolves got in or why they only came when Father was gone.

Part of the fence went along the road. There was not much traffic. One day I happened to be walking in the same direction as a boy who was walking away from town. He had brown skin and darker brown hair and wore red trousers. He carried a bundle and waved hello to me. He

was not wearing a hat. I waved hello back.

The next day I saw him again. This time he spoke to me: "Hello," he said, waving again. He wore the same red trousers and no hat. I smiled and said "Hello" back.

Every day we said hello as we walked next to each other, separated by my fence. On Saturday he was not there. On Sunday he was not there. On Monday he was back, and I knew he must go to school in town. I leaned on the fence and called to him. "Hello. What are you carrying?"

He came over to me and said, "I am carrying my books. Do you live here?"

"Yes," I told him. "I'm Erzsébet."

"Are you a Penderghast?" he asked.

"Yes, sort of. My mother was a Penderghast. My grandmother is a Penderghast. My father and I are Trnkas."

"I'm Jeet," he responded. "Jeet Acharya."

After that we spoke every afternoon. The moon went black, then began to wax again. As she grew, I came to dread the three days when Father would go away and I would be confined with Grandmother, who might be mad.

I confided in Jeet without telling him everything.

"Father goes away every month and I am afraid of the wolves."

"He goes away? Why?"

I could not answer Jeet. I did not know.

○

By the time Father went away again, Grandmother could get herself from her bed to her chair, and could use the chamber pot. Father brought her back to her room in the tower, though I was frightened because I could not carry her downstairs from there. Father assured me nothing would go wrong. I did not believe him, but I could not contradict him.

In a way I was glad, because the tower was far from the wolves.

I brought Grandmother her dinner of bread and cabbage and roasted lamb. She pushed the meat aside and ate the bread.

"Don't you feel well, Grandmother? You always loved lamb."

"I can't hear the wolves," she answered, and I didn't know what to say.

"I'll leave your plate in case you get hungry later," I told her, and I went downstairs in the twilight. The wolves were starting to come toward the house, circling and looking in at the windows. I could have sworn the big one was looking for Grandmother. I went to the window and he pushed his nose against the glass. I reached out and touched the glass, and I felt a spark course through me. I snatched back my hand and stood staring at the wolf in the window until I recovered my senses.

I drew the curtains.

In the morning Grandmother rang her bell and I ran to her room. I found her sitting in bed, her hair down, soft grey curls cascading over her shoulders. She looked beautiful, but so thin and sallow, with light spots sprinkled across her nose and cheeks, some of them larger and browner now she is older. Grandmother was a beauty, or so she tells me.

"Are you ready for your breakfast?" I asked her.

"Porridge," she said. "Bring me my teeth."

We had never spoken of the drawer of teeth, and I did not know how she knew that I knew of it. I carefully removed the drawer from her dresser and brought it to her, trying not to look at the dozens and dozens of loose teeth that filled it. There might have been hundreds.

I ran downstairs and prepared Grandmother's porridge, along with my own. Milk and honey. The last of the butter until spring. Stewed apples. Soon we would tire of apples, but for now we had plenty of sugar and fat to bake them with. The lambs do not give much fat, but the pigs filled our stores with all we could need. We do not raise the animals ourselves; the wolves would eat them. We buy them every year and see them raised in town, then have them slaughtered and the meat cured to Father's exact specifications.

When I returned, Grandmother had ar-ranged the teeth in little half moons all over her bed. Most of the mouths had too many cuspids, the second sets too large for the rest of the teeth.

I set Grandmother's breakfast on her table and helped her over to it.

"Do you see my teeth?" she asked me, and I tried not to scream.

"Where did you get so many teeth, Grand-mother?" I asked, though I did not want to know the answer.

"I collected them," she told me, and I did not know the answer. "My mother collected them before me," she added, and I still did not know the answer.

We ate together and I knitted while she showed me each set of teeth and told me who it belonged to. One was Mother's, with an extra set of cuspids. One was mine, little pearl-like baby teeth with only one set of cuspids. One she said was Robert's; I still did not know who Robert was. He only had one set of cuspids.

Then she swept all the teeth together in the center of her bed, running her fingers through them. Her cheeks were rosier and her skin glowed a healthy golden.

"Do you remember your mother, Bözsi?" No one had called me Bözsi since I was very small.

"No," I told her, but I did not know if it was true. Sometimes I thought I remembered her and other times I was sure my memories were only the stories I'd been told. Stories I'd heard that were not meant for my ears.

Mother ran off.

Mother died.

Mother disappeared.

The stories were not always nice stories.

I knew—whether from memory or from stories and pictures, I could not say—that Mother was beautiful, with long red hair and covered in freckles. I took after Father, dark and plain.

"Your uncle Robert was my first. He died before your mother came."

I did not know how to answer her in her renewed grief.

O

That afternoon while Grandmother was asleep I sneaked out to see Jeet. He rode a bicycle that day and leaned against the fence still straddling it.

"Father is away," I told him in a hushed voice. I did not tell him about my uncle.

"Does he go away every month at the full moon?" Jeet asked me, and I nodded.

"Don't you know what this means?" he asked, and I shook my head no.

"I'll tell you tomorrow," Jeet said, pedaling off toward his home.

"Wait!" I called after him, but he was already gone. I was not ready for him to go. When he was near me I felt something like hunger in my belly.

The next day I lost track of time finishing my knitting project and was late to meet Jeet. He was not there, but there was a package on the fence wrapped in brown paper with ERZIBET written on it in pencil. I tore off the paper and found a book. It was small and bound in what might have been leather. I left Jeet's gift, a knitted hat, on a fence post, and took the book home and hid it under my pillow. When Grandmother was asleep, I read by candlelight and the light of the moon. The book seemed to be the story of a woman whose husband disappeared every month at the full moon. The story was told by a doctor who was treating the woman for madness, only the woman was not mad. Her husband was turning into a monster every month.

Was Jeet trying to tell me that my father went away every full moon to turn into a monster? I could not believe it, but then, why else would Father have given me the book about Mr. Hyde? Why else would Grandmother have insisted that he go, even when she was so ill? I could not account for his taking Grandmother's nurse with him, unless perhaps he needed the nurse's help in some way. To keep from losing his mind, perhaps. Or his soul. I was not sure how such things worked.

The next day Jeet was wearing the hat I'd left for him, and I was glad. I asked him about the book and he said that Father was a werewolf.

"I don't believe it," I told him, although I did. I did not want to believe it.

"You must," he told me. And I did.

"Is there any silver in your house?"

"Ye-eesss," I said, suddenly unsure. "No. I don't know!"

"What do you eat with?"

I described Grandmother's flatware and the patina that I polished off the serving ladle every year at Yuletide.

"Copper or brass," he told me. I nodded.

"What about photographs?"

I admitted that we had none. I knew my mother's face only from the painting in Father's room.

"Mirrors?"

"We have one of those! It hangs on the landing."

"Well," he told me, "it sounds like that is the only silver in the house. Definitely *were*."

O

When Father returned I could not stand to look at him.

I found that when Father was at home, I was not hungry. He worried, but Grandmother was unconcerned. "She is almost a woman," she reminded Father.

I spent more time in Grandmother's tower, sorting and resorting her teeth. She told me stories about each set. Some of them seemed like fairy stories. One child, many generations ago, was born with a full set of teeth. Another grew no teeth at all until well into childhood. Some of the stories were sad, others funny. She never told me any stories at all about Mother's teeth. I held Mother's extra cuspids in the palm of my hand like pearls.

O

That month the wolves came on the night of the

new moon. I looked out the window but did not see the large wolf who sometimes came to the window. Father drew the curtains and spoke to Grandmother in hushed tones when he thought I could not hear him. I could not make out his words, but I knew they were about me.

That night I dreamed about the wolves. I was alone in the woods, looking for them. I walked silently, my footfalls making no sound on the soft ground cover. The wolves found me and I followed them as they ran free through the woods. I thought I glimpsed a woman in their midst, naked and wild, with huge tangles of grey and red and brown hair on her head and surrounding her body, which was pale and spotted with brown. I woke gasping for air and pulled a hairball from my tongue.

The next ten days were the loneliest of my life. Father did not speak to me and Grandmother seemed distant. My stomach felt empty, though I was not hungry; my back ached.

I climbed the stairs to Grandmother's tower and asked her to tell me about Mother's teeth. She shook her head no and instead showed me mine.

"Your new teeth will come soon," she told me.

"No, Grandmother," I answered. "I have all of my teeth."

She looked out the window for a long time, silent, before answering. "I was older than you when I got mine," she said. "I had such a short time to use them. My change came so early. You were still a baby. It was before your mother left—"

She shut her mouth then and would not speak again.

On the morning that Father was to go away, I woke with a terrible pain in my mouth and a fire in my belly. I sat up and found three cuspids on my pillow, stained red. I stood and found a small pool of blood on my sheets, my undergarments soaked through. I felt a lump in my mouth and reached into it, pulling the fourth cuspid off my swollen tongue. I pulled on my dressing gown, gathered the teeth in my handkerchief, and walked down to the landing, where I gazed into the mirror. It was the only mirror in the entire house, and looking into it directly hurt my eyes. I opened my mouth and a hideous grin looked back at me, with four new, sharp teeth in the spaces where my cuspids had been.

My new teeth.

I went to the kitchen and took the kettle from the fire. I carried it to the landing and swung it in a wide arc, smashing the mirror into smithereens. The shards covered the stairs. I brushed them from my nightgown and they stung my hands.

I brought my old cuspids to Grandmother for her collection.

Father did not go away that night. He cleaned up the shards of the mirror, keeping me away from the mess with his booming voice ordering me to stay upstairs.

As the sun set, he and Grandmother called me to the great hall, where the stairs framed the front door and the tile floor subtly suggested the family crest.

"It is time, Bözsi," Father said. "You are a Penderghast now." Grandmother reached out and squeezed my hand.

Then Father opened the great front door and pushed me out, slamming it behind me. I heard the lock fall into place. I leaned back against the door, sobbing in terror. When I finally looked up, I saw the moon in all her fullness, a lady in her evening gown, shining down just for me. The wolves had come silently and were in their ring around the house. The large wolf was there. She came forward, right up to me. I knew her then.

"Mother?" I asked, and my transformation was upon me.

WEIRD HOUSE

a specialty horror press

Order from weirdhousepress.com

WHENEVER IT COMES

☙❧

STEVE RASNIC TEM

It was a long year of quiet dread. I lost my job. I lost my nerve. I stayed home and watched over the house and my family. I made my wife uncomfortable, but I believed she knew I had their best interests in mind.

At first, I saw no one outside, not even the neighbors. They kept their curtains closed. Sometimes I could hear their children screaming inside. I had no idea if theirs was an expression of bottled-up excitement or pain. My own children remained as still and quiet as possible. I asked them to pretend they did not exist. I wanted people to believe no one lived here anymore. Sometimes I believed it myself.

It broke my heart trying to keep our children safe. I didn't want to tell them the world had become a dangerous place. As parents we made mistakes, sometimes terrible mistakes, as all parents will. Yet our children still looked to us for answers.

I didn't understand how things worked anymore. I didn't believe anyone did. I no longer trusted people, least of all myself. No one knew for sure what lived inside the human heart. No one knew how this would end.

The air went from beige to gray to nothing at all. Sometimes we could see distant cities and mountain ranges and the possibilities which lay beyond. No one had ever seen such skies, and we gazed at them from our windows, hoping we were safe behind the glass. The sun could see everything and shone its bright judgement across the world. The animals came out of the woods and nibbled on the edges of civilization. Pets retreated inside and refused to leave.

Unable to bear our solitude, some of us exited our homes and wandered the sidewalks. I spoke to no one. Our neighbors appeared changed. I told my wife and children to stay inside and never, ever, answer the door. I was embarrassed by my words. Sometimes I didn't recognize my own thoughts. I didn't want to give orders to anyone, but it was a time of desperate behavior.

My father was one of those who fell ill. My elderly mother was hysterical and spoke nonsense over the phone. I was afraid of what might happen to my family while I was gone. I explained again to my wife and children what to do if there was a knock on the door. Stay inside. Whatever you do don't answer. I took a long and circuitous route to my parents' house, without stopping and avoiding the major population centers. When I arrived, I learned my father was dead.

My mother and I were the only ones at my father's graveside service. Others stood watching from a distance. Some seemed familiar, but they were too far away to know for sure. Where did these spectators come from? None had been invited. After the funeral my mother came to live with us. Her house sold quickly, and she chose to trash most of her possessions rather than see them go into a thrift store. She said she needed nothing at this point, nothing at all.

My father wanted to come too, but my father was dead. So I told him no. That he would even ask made me angry. I had my children to consider.

We drove for miles without seeing another car. When we did encounter another vehicle, I slowed down for a better view. The people inside were never what I expected. They stared at us as if we were the strange ones.

Once home I searched the house to see if anything had changed. I asked my wife if there were visitors while I was gone but her answers seemed evasive. My children acted as if I'd never left them. They ignored my mother and continued to play with their invisible toys.

The city stopped picking up our garbage. They lied when they claimed basic services would not be affected. Food continued to be delivered. They would leave it on the front step, and I retrieved it when I thought no one was watching. Whatever packaging or scraps were left I buried in the backyard. Sometimes I thought my neighbors were watching me from behind their curtains. Sometimes it seemed everyone was holding their breath.

I could not remember the last time I saw a plane in the sky, but the air was full of birds, sometimes so many they collided, and their dead bodies hit the house in syncopating drumbeats. I told my children it was hail and to stay away from the windows.

Every morning I insisted we make some feeble attempt at normalcy. We all sat at the kitchen table for breakfast. My son Billy was infected with a new frenetic energy and could not sit still. He kept getting out of his chair, walking around the kitchen, and prattled on about this, that, and everything else. My mother, who listened intently, both smiled and frowned at random. My little daughter Caroline remained silent. She had not spoken in over a year.

My wife left the table and walked down the hall to the living room. She asked if I would join her there. She said there was something important she needed to tell me.

I didn't want to leave. This was supposed to be our family time. Billy was telling my mother a long and complicated tale. She smiled and nodded but I didn't think she understood anything he was saying. Caroline stared at her pancakes and sausage, the steam rolling off them in waves and dissipating into the bright kitchen air. I worried she might be starving herself.

I left the table to join my wife. As my mother was the only remaining adult, she was now in charge of the kitchen. I walked down the hall to the front of the house. I felt a powerful urge to turn around and look at my children.

My wife was talking but I couldn't focus on what she was saying. I glanced down the hallway into the kitchen. My mother was sitting with her back to me. I heard the sharp rise and fall of my son Billy's voice. I could not see Caroline.

My wife told me she needed help keeping the house clean and orderly the way I liked it. She said I had to stop staring out the windows and making everyone nervous. She needed help keeping things organized, especially now the entire family was home all the time. She needed help in the garden. She told me the garden was like a jungle and the yard was almost as bad.

I said "I thought we agreed we wouldn't be going outside anymore. Don't tell me you've been going outside."

Someone knocked on the back door.

"Don't answer it!" I shouted. "Mother, Billy, don't answer the door!"

My wife kept talking. I had a hard time giving her my attention. I didn't catch all her words. There's something else I must tell you, she said.

Someone knocked on the back door again. "Don't answer!" I cried. I saw Caroline cross behind the table headed toward the back door. "Billy, don't let your sister answer the door!"

I started toward the kitchen, but my wife held my arm. A few days ago, my wife continued, when you were napping, someone came to the door.

"*Tell me* you didn't answer it. Just tell me that."

It was a man, just an ordinary man, she said. He wanted directions to the Willis's. I pointed to the house across the street, and I closed the door. That's all. Nothing else happened. Everything is perfectly fine.

I heard the back door open. I heard my son, still chattering on. My wife said I know I shouldn't have, but everything's fine. Everything is perfectly fine.

"Mother? Who's there? Don't let him inside!"

I know I shouldn't have, my wife kept saying.

I heard those big shoes, and then Billy calling Dad! Dad! The Shut-Up Man is Here!

But my wife was still talking, trying to explain herself. I kept hearing those big shoes moving around, and Billy had stopped talking altogether, and my mother was no longer in her chair.

My wife said she knew she shouldn't have opened the door. Where was Caroline? My wife said it was one little mistake. But everything was perfectly fine.

"Shut up shut up shut up!" I shouted, with fists clenched and eyes closed. I shouted this over and over until the house was quiet again.

I turned to my wife to apologize but the front door was open, and my wife was not there. I gazed into the kitchen, but the kitchen appeared empty. That's when I realized this house was no longer ours, but belonged to whomever, or whatever, comes after, whenever it comes.

HURLED AGAINST ROCKS

CallBD

ANDREW HUMPHREY

I'm in Waterstones, lost in the Crime and Horror, when I see Holly. She's a couple of aisles across, scanning the rear of a paperback. Five years have passed since our agonising disentanglement. She's changed. Her hair, once blonde and long is now red and very short. She is incredibly slim. She's dressed simply and stylishly; tight jeans, a pale lemon sleeveless blouse.

I'm deep in the Stephen King's, holding a hardback copy of *Insomnia* limply in my right hand. I've already stared at her for too long so I try to plot the best route to the store's exit. Desperate to avoid her attention I attempt to slide the book back in place before making my escape. I drop it of course and it clatters to the floor. A number of heads turn towards me. Holly's is one of them. It takes her a moment to register that it's me and then she mouths a solitary word. "Fuck."

The book she's looking at is *Waterland* by Graham Swift. She carries it as she walks towards me.

"Daniel? Well I never."

Daniel? I'm Dan. I'd always been Dan. "Holly. You look great."

She nods. She's close. Too close? Probably. She smells fantastic though. When she speaks her breath puffs against my face. "You're back?"

"Mum died."

"I know."

"I'm trying to sell her place. I'm kind of living there."

"Living there? What happened to London?"

The tiniest fleck of spittle strikes my chin. It's warm. "It didn't really work out."

She relaxes a fraction and eases away from me. Glancing down she seems surprised to see the book in her right hand.

"He's very good," I say. "Swift. *Light of Day* is excellent. You'd love it."

Her head tilts to one side and she looks at me without expression. "We should have a coffee," she says.

We should? "What? Now?"

"Why not?"

I can think of a whole host of reasons but it seems that I cannot articulate them. Instead I say, "Okay," and follow her out of the store.

○

There's a Costa across the street and we walk towards it. The early summer sky is clear and pale. The air is warm and it feels good to retreat into the coffee shop's shaded, air-conditioned interior.

Holly orders herself a coffee. The barista tries to flirt with her but she looks at him blankly. When he turns my way I ask for a flat white. He doesn't flirt with me. We pay separately and find a seat by the window.

Holly sips her black coffee carefully then places the cup very precisely back on the saucer and links her fingers together on the table in front of her.

"You look great," I say.

"Why do you think we're here?" She turns her gaze towards me. Her eyes are a shade of hazel. They were warm once, I seem to recall, but now they are cold and empty. "I mean, look at me. And look at you."

I glance down involuntarily; I see the frayed collar of my Dry the River t-shirt and below that, a swelling paunch. I haven't shaved or showered for a couple of days. Other than that; gorgeous. "I wasn't expecting company."

"I was fat, now I'm thin."

"You weren't fat, Holly."

"I was fat." She presses her hands together in front of her face, as though in prayer. "Now I'm thin."

"You weren't … and that wasn't why I left."

"So you said." Another sip of coffee, another rearrangement of hands and fingers. "And how is the writing? No bestseller? Unless you're using a pen name, of course?"

"No bestseller," I say quietly. No *any* seller. No agent. No ideas. No hope.

"Oh dear. And don't tell me you didn't even *find* yourself?"

"I never said anything about *finding* myself. I'm not a complete dick." It seems that I've dredged a little anger from somewhere and her eyes flick onto mine.

"No. You didn't say anything. It was kind of implied."

Of course it was implied. That's the whole point of being passive aggressive; *everything's* implied. You never actually *say* anything. I stand. "Well, this has been lovely."

"Leaving so soon?"

"You've made your point."

"I'm not sure I have a point."

"I'm a bastard. I ruined your life."

"You didn't ruin my life," she says quietly. Her hands are on the move again, fingertips steepled beneath her chin.

Her gaze seems fixed on my navel and I tug my t-shirt down self-consciously. But she's looking through me not at me. I wonder idly, briefly, if this is actually Holly at all. Perhaps it's a doppelganger or a replicant. Maybe. It would make as much sense as anything these days. "I've got to go," I say.

"Of course you have."

I leave her again. She stares at a spot on the wall opposite as something by Simon and Garfunkel washes gently across the half-empty room.

○

We stood in the graveyard at Heydon Church. This was years ago; we were freshly engaged and still bright and shiny with love. Or, at least, the chemical miasma that passes as such. I was idly wandering amongst the gravestone, noting the names. I sometimes used them in my writing.

"Grix," I said. "That's a great name. I'm nicking that."

Holly came to my side. She smelled of heather and sun cream. "Sounds a bit Dickensian."

"Would have to be a baddie, I think." I patted the worn edge of the stone, which felt warm in the hard August sun. "No offence."

I stood and Holly slid a hand into mine. She pressed her shoulder against me. She wore a jacket over a summery top, in spite of the heat. It kept her covered up, she said, self-conscious as she was about her weight. I told her she was being silly, which, on reflection, probably wasn't very helpful.

"Do you think they do weddings here?"

We were stood next to the church's southern wall, the village green behind us. The ancient stonework looked resplendent, awash with light.

"What?"

"Your face," Holly said, squinting at me, a hand shielding her eyes. "It's not such an unreasonable question. We'll be getting married somewhere, I assume."

"Of course. Sorry. It's not that local, though. Not really."

She let me flounder a little then laughed and said, "It's fine, I just wondered that's all. It's such a beautiful setting."

"Nearly as beautiful as you."

She snorted. "Nice try. It'll take more than that though. Mr Romantic."

I pointed at the coffee shop across the road. "I

could treat you to a cream tea?"

"That's more like it." She squeezed my hand. "It's okay. There's plenty of time for wedding plans. I'm only teasing." As we walked our hips bumped together. "And Mum...well, you know. She does go on a bit."

"I know," I said, but my mind was already drifting. The story I was writing had run aground and the trip to the church had nothing to do with future wedding plans. It was about research, atmosphere, and an attempt at a creative jolt.

It hadn't really worked.

Holly was warm and kind. A day in her company was a pleasure. No doubt we'd go to bed later and she'd exhibit her warmth and kindness all over again. I was a lucky man, as I told myself over and over. As did my friends and Holly's family and, occasionally, Holly herself.

On reflection, though, I wished I'd visited the church alone.

○

It's late by the time I get back to my mother's terraced house on Lincoln Street. Actually it's my house now, has been since her death, but I find it difficult to think of it that way. It's still crammed with her belongings. She became a hoarder in her later years and I have neither the will nor the energy to even begin sorting through the decades of impacted detritus. I keep the living room tidy enough. I sleep on the sofa. I've cleared a path through the stacks of *Family Circles* and *Eastern Evening News* to the kitchen and bathroom. I hardly venture upstairs at all.

I was late because I'd eaten at McDonald's then lingered over a couple of pints in the York on the way home. I'd tried to read but the sentences blurred and then stumbled together. I thought of Holly and felt shame and a familiar, numbing sense of inertia. I came home eventually to a house that was stuck in time and to a life that is so stunted and frozen it may as well be set in amber.

○

I started writing fiction at school. It was our English teacher's fault. Mr Bolting. He was kind, encouraging, patient. I was reading mostly Dad's hand-me-downs; paperbacks by MacLean, Robbins, Haley. I told Mr Bolting and he shrugged and said, nothing wrong with that. Then he wrote a list of names. But why not try these as well; Greene, Malamud, Roth, Nabokov, Lurie, Heller. I loved them all except Roth. Mr Bolting said he wasn't much to his taste either and suggested Woolf, Orwell, Atwood.

He set us tasks as well, outside of the usual curriculum. Most of the class groaned but I loved them. Handing back one piece—a thousand words with a twist at the end—he tapped my shoulder and said, a hint of genius there, Daniel.

I glowed then. I felt immense. Until I got home and told Mum and said that I was going to be a writer. That's nice, love, she said. You write your little stories, but remember you've still got to get a proper job. Norwich Union are always hiring though. They'll probably take you.

I ate my tea in silence. I was back to the normal size. Perhaps I was even a little smaller.

○

I watch some TV—a documentary about Hemingway. It's probably excellent but I doze for a while twenty minutes in and then can't really pick up the thread. I've never read any Hemingway. I feel as though I should but I've never quite got around to it. What I do gather from the program is that he was a prick. Talented though. I'm confident that I have the prick part nailed down; the talent bit is proving more elusive. I let the wave of self-pity have its way with me—it's addictive and oddly pleasurable after all—then make my bed on the sofa and fall asleep.

The voice that wakes me is light and familiar. "I like what you've done with the place."

I sit upright, cricking my neck. "Holly. Jesus Christ." There's little light and I can sense rather than see her. "What are you doing?"

"The front door was open."

"That's not an answer. I mean, what the actual fuck?" I struggle into a sitting position. The air is fetid and my mouth tastes foul.

"You're not a bastard. It's not your fault that I am ... how I am." I'm getting used to the light now and I can see Holly's outline. She's knelt on the floor, close to the sofa, her head angled towards me. I claw my way through the outrage and disorientation and try to formulate a response. I become aware of the rankness of my scent and breath. "You did abandon me, though, Dan. You just did."

"I know, Holly. I know."

"But the weight ... well, that was Mum. She was always on at me about it, ever since I was little."

"It was never ..."

"I know." Her voice had become soft but it sharpens now as she cuts me off. "I know, Dan. I guess I wasn't quite enough, that's the long and short of it. And I can't blame you for that, can I? Not really."

"Look ..." I feel her hand, cool against my forearm, stilling me.

"She called me a fat cow. Can you believe that?" Actually I can. "Said I'd never get a man looking like I did. Said that was why you left. So it was something, wasn't it? Something I could control. A way of shutting her up."

"Okay," I say slowly. I stand and flick on a lamp. It's a little after five. Holly blinks up at me. She's wearing the same clothes as earlier. "I'm sorry. For everything. Really. But you can't do this. You can't just ..."

"I thought you needed to know. It wasn't your fault."

"So it was your mum's ..."

She cuts me off again as she stands. "No. I'm slim because of her. I suppose I should thank

her, really."

"Then what the ..."

"It's your brother, Dan. He's the bastard." Her head flicks from side to side as she surveys the wreckage of this awful room.

A chill forms inside me. "My brother's dead, Holly."

"Well, I know that," she says as she faces me. She's too close again and her smile is too wide. "I'm not silly."

○

Everyone loved Jacob. Even Dad, in his distant, ineffectual way. And Mum... well, Mum... I suppose smitten is the word. He *was* adorable, on the face of it, at least, with his blue eyes and his curly blond hair and his dimpled grin. He was the youngest by three years. He took all of my space and light. He didn't even try; he just mopped it up with his laugh and his smile and his off-centre charm. God, I hated him. On the beach at Cromer, during our annual visit, I'd take an hour or two making ugly, functional sandcastles and he'd toddle up and sweep them aside with his plastic spade and his stupid high-pitched laugh and Mum and Dad would chuckle along with him and so would the family next to us and I'd look at his gormless, gummy, white-toothed smile and imagine holding his golden, tousled head under the shallow surf until he was finally quiet. Perhaps then he would leave me alone. I was eight, I suppose, Jacob five.

"Look at your brother," Mum would say, "Isn't he clever."

"Good old, Jake," I'd say, my smile a horrible, frozen thing. "Clever Jake."

○

When we were older he read one of my stories.

It had been picked up by a half-decent independent magazine so I was feeling pretty good about it.

"This is shit, mate."

"What?"

We were living at home still, the two of us. We were in the living room; Dralon three-piece, heavy flock wallpaper. Mum and Dad were out.

"It just is. It's so fucking dull."

"It's gritty. Urban."

"Who the fuck wants to read that?" He rubbed his fingers together. "Where's the dosh? They won't make a movie out of this."

"It's not all about …"

"Look. I can put a word in for you. At work. Get you out of that shithole team."

We were both at Norwich Union—of course we were—but he'd charmed his way up a couple of ladders while I was grubbing around in claims, in the basement, mopping up all the crap.

"No, thanks."

He clapped me on the back. "Your funeral." He tossed the magazine to me but I dropped it and it fell to the floor. "Anyway, I've got to go, mate. People to do, things to see."

He gave me a hammy wink and left in a cloud of Blue Stratos.

○

When I started dating Holly, Jake was single.

"Too good for you, mate," he said, in the kitchen, Holly left to fend for herself with Mum and Dad in the living room, which was stressful enough as it was.

"Please fuck off."

He held his arms wide, all mock offence, his smile pure charm, his hair still blond and unruly, his shoulders broad. He was taller than me too, which really didn't help. "Easy, tiger. She's not my type."

"They're all your type, Jake."

"Some of us can afford to be discerning." It was a quiet, sly dig, borne out by facts. It left its mark, as he knew it would.

Actually, Holly didn't like him. She found him shallow and irritating. This undoubtedly added to her initial attraction. "I wonder if he's gay?" she said once and it was then that I knew that I loved her.

○

There's an independent coffee shop recently opened near me—Danish, vegan, achingly trendy. I finally usher Holly out of the house and we agree to meet there later in the morning.

I shower and shave and change my clothes. I clean my teeth. I'm really making an effort.

Holly isn't. When I get to the coffee shop she's waiting outside in the same clothes as earlier. The day is bright and warm and she seems diminished by it. When I draw close to her there's an odd, bitter edge to her scent.

I order for both of us this time and we settle into small pine chairs in the corner of the room. The drinks come quickly, flat whites made with oat milk.

"I had this feeling you'd be vegan," I say.

"I'm not. This is fine though."

"I wonder why I thought that?"

"No idea, Dan. It's not even any of your business, is it?"

"Fair point. Although you did break into my house in the early hours and start raving about my dead brother, so all bets are off now, really, aren't they?"

She sips her drink, leaving a line of foam on her upper lip. I remember kissing that mouth once. It seems odd now, but then it seems odd that I ever touched her at all. "I didn't break in. The door was unlocked. And I wasn't raving."

"Is this a joke, Holly? Is this your way of getting back at me?"

She releases a long outward breath. We are sitting opposite each other and there's an empty chair to Holly's left. She reaches out a hand and strokes the back of the chair and nods towards it. "He's here now."

My gaze snaps involuntarily towards the empty seat. "What?"

"He looks pretty good, all things considered. He's looking at you. He's got that leather jacket on, the black one? Pretty hot really."

"Hot? You said you didn't ..."

"I said a lot of things. We both did. And I think you're missing the point."

"The point?"

She frowns suddenly and deeply. "He looks angry. He looks furious, Dan. He's reaching for you."

Something cold slides from my stomach towards my chest. The coffee machines hiss loudly, drowning out the soft, folksy music playing in the background. "Stop this, Holly. Stop it now."

"It's not up to me. I've had five years of this. Every fucking day. Out of nowhere. By my side at work, when I'm jogging. In my bed, his voice wet in my ear. He remembers the taste of me, he says. Being inside me."

Her voice has become robotic. She's staring at the empty chair and I'm staring at her. "What are you saying? Do you mean ..."

"You're the bastard, aren't you, Jake?" As far as I can see she's speaking to dead air, but her head snaps back and her expression changes, as though she's received a reply. "You're missing the point again, Dan." She looks at me. She appears demented. "You always miss the point."

"I don't have to take this."

"Neither do I. He's your brother. I need you to make him stop."

○

In my life, for the longest time, very little happened. Then for a handful of days, in spring, five years ago, it all kicked off.

On the morning of our wedding I sent a text to Holly telling her I couldn't go through with it. Then I turned my phone off and drove to London. I had an acquaintance, a former colleague from Norwich Union who had moved on to better things. He said I could use his sofa in a crisis. He seemed a little surprised when I

took him up on the offer but he was as good as his word.

In my mind—what passed for my mind— Holly was holding me back. If I was going to make it as a writer I needed to be independent and to live in London. I was being published widely in the independent press at this point and had attracted the attentions of an agent; London based, of course, new and keen and seeking fresh young voices to join his stable. It was only a matter of time, I thought; book launches, tours, an interview in the Guardian. I had it all mapped out.

I just needed to make the break.

Later that I evening I turned my phone on again. I deleted most of the messages unread. I sent a long text to Holly trying to explain my decision. I think there was an apology in there somewhere. I hope so.

There was also a voice message from Jake. I did listen to that.

"You dopey prick. What the fuck are you playing at? You can't do this. You can't ... let her down. She's too good for you. I told you that. Too good for all of us." There was a pause as he tried to contain his anger. His breathing became ragged. "I know where you've gone. It's Paul, isn't it? Nearly as soppy as you. Well, I'm coming to get you, big brother. I'm going to come and get you and drag you back here." Another pause and then his voice again, crawling towards me. "As for Mum ... you'll be the death of her, you know that, don't you? You dopey, *dopey* prick."

I looked at the phone. For some reason I played the message again and didn't delete it. Paul was out, I sat on his sofa in his neat, small living room and listened to my brother's voice, to his fury and indignation and waited for him to come.

It turns out he was already dead. He'd ploughed his Escort into the back of a stationary lorry on the A11 about two hours earlier and was killed instantly. I didn't go to the funeral. Three weeks later my dad had a fatal heart attack. I didn't go to his funeral either.

○

I get us some more coffees. I don't know what else to do.

When I get back to my seat Holly's expression has eased and she's slumped back in her chair. "He's gone."

"Okay."

"I know how this sounds."

"Did you fuck him, Holly?"

Her smile is slow and acidic. "You really need to rein in the indignation there, Dan."

"I can't believe you fucked him."

"I thought you knew. We weren't even that careful." Her voice is easy and casual and it surprises me how much this hurts. "I thought it would be useful for you. For your writing; you know, grist to the mill. It was all you cared about, after all."

"Seriously?"

"Everyone thought I was sweet little Holly. Butter wouldn't melt. I was so sick of it."

"Is that why he's haunting you? Because you fucked him?"

"What, are you jealous of that as well?" She lifts her coffee cup then puts it down again. "How do I know? Anyway, you weren't here, were you? You'd run away, hadn't you? From everything and everyone. For all the good it did you."

"Well, I'm here now."

"Indeed you are."

○

I met the agent once, in a bar on Balham High Street. Nice guy. A bit distracted though. It was clearly never going to work, for him or for me. Apparently he's in real estate now. Norwich Union found me a position in a sub-office off Streatham High Street; claims, of course. I was lucky they kept me on, I suppose. I was lucky also to find a flat, once Paul's patience had finally expired. It was an appalling place and I had to share with a strung out ex drug dealer and his succession of burnt out, borderline abusive partners. Still ... should have been grist to the mill, I suppose, as Holly would say. Life's rich tapestry laid out before me. What more could a writer want? Except I was so utterly blocked it made no difference at all. I haven't written a single word since my brother died. Not a word. Until now.

○

Outside the café Holly brushes off my offer to walk her home with wordless contempt. I'm pleased as I don't really mean it. She does hug me, though, which is quite a surprise. It seems odd, the leanness of her body against mine.

"I feel lighter," she says. "I think he's gone."

I'm not sure what to say to that so I say nothing.

I think she's about to leave but instead she says, "There's no point being *nice*, is there?" She emphasises the word "nice," extends it to its limits. "No point in being decent, kind. May as well be a prick, like you."

"Okay."

"What difference does it make? We're all just hurled against rocks, aren't we? At the end of the day?"

"Fuck's sake, Holly."

She shrugs and now she does leave, turning on her heel and marching towards the city centre, head down, shoulders hunched against the world.

○

I stand for a while then walk in the opposite direction. I find a newsagent and buy a pad and a cheap biro. I find another coffee shop and sit at a window table, just like I used to years ago, and I write and write and write.

○

The light is fading when I finish, my wrist aches and my mind feels scoured clean. As I walk home the air feels tired and re-used and difficult to breathe. The house is hushed, waiting. I've barely eaten all day but it doesn't seem to matter. I watch some TV as the evening dies.

I make my bed and lie in it. Don't we all? I wait for sleep to come and the only surprise is that it does.

That I wake again before dawn is no surprise at all. I breathe in the thick night air and listen. I hear the creak of cheap leather and catch the acrylic scent of even cheaper after shave.

The voice is wet and warm in my ear.

"You dopey prick," my brother says.

FIELDS AND SCATTER

☙❧

ASHLEY STOKES

First sight of the only off-screen, flesh-and-blood-woman for nearly a year tingled his stomach. He crossed the glistening forecourt. She was hiding behind a pillar. This was sensible, despite their rendezvousing at a dilapidated garage in the dead of nowhere. It was sensible, too, that she had brought a dog. It strained on a short leash, some sort of terrier, by the looks of it. Her face was obscured by a khaki-green hood. She was, though—and had been—real.

It had been her choice to meet here, an oil-stained oblong of cement with an abandoned shack of a shop plonked upon it. Across the road, wet fields, a jagged line of bronze-coloured trees and a curtain of misty rain. On his drive over, no other cars used the roads. No machines or people worked the fields. He saw no one in the lane where she had told him to park up away from the garage. She'd told him the name—Bruton's—and joked that he would never find it, as if catching her here was some sort of test.

The dog reared up. She pulled down her hood. She wasn't wearing a mask. He took his off. This was a matter of trust.

"There's no one else here," he said, "so it must be you." He wished he'd said something that hinted they were breaking the rules to take a shot at impossible romance.

"So, you make it?" she said.

Good. She'd said something clunky and obvious, too. English was her second language. He hadn't expected witty wordplay. A relief: he was crap at banter. He wondered what a nice Finnish girl like her was doing in a place like this. He wouldn't ask her this now. He would save it for later. It was a good line. He mustn't waste it.

Her eyes seemed to glint with a violet flash. For a second he thought that a car may have whooshed by, but when he turned, the road was clear both ways.

She was in her mid-thirties, like her profile said, and she had blonde hair neatly tied with a black scrunchie. She wore walking boots, black leggings, some sort of short, hip-hugging black skirt and a denim jacket over her hoodie. She actually looked like her profile picture. Several of the women he had met for dates before the Great Disorder had been using pictures so old they still had Rachel from *Friends* hairstyles. Vemi appeared exactly like he had imagined. In her profile, which had not been up for very long, only a couple of days, she described herself as an events organiser. When he'd first contacted her, he asked her what sort of event she would like to organise if they were to go on a date? This must have shown more engagement with her on a human level than, say, asking, "do you want a dumb arse to go with your nice arse?" even though Nigel from Compliance one night in in the pub had said that line was solid gold. He had used it on Tarsh from Design and the temp in Accounts he called JoJo Binks.

After a few friendly messages, Vemi had disabled her profile. Now they were meeting up. Her dog was nosing its way across the road. Her dog was pulling her behind it as it scampered alongside the hedge that protected the field. He was following her and her dog away from Bruton's Garage.

He caught up and tried to put himself between her and the road. They were exposed out here and had not agreed on a cover story should they be seen by an Eye-Spy or Disorder Reporter. Neither of them spoke. A kind of guilt swallowed him. He felt innocent, yet unable to represent himself, like he had at school when Roberto threw that wooden block at Mattock's head in Old Gill's woodwork class and he had somehow been blamed and punished. These things linger. These things scar.

Vemi tugged on the lead to yank the dog out of the hedge where he was attacking a Twix wrapper. He really wasn't sure what sort of dog it was. His "some sort of terrier" observation needed revision to "some sort of four-legged mammal."

"What's his name?" he asked.

"Gufo," she said.

"I don't think I've met a dog called Gufo before."

"There's only one Gufo."

"What breed is he?"

She laughed. "Like I say, there is only one Gufo."

"So," he said, "what's a nice Finnish girl like you doing in a place like this?"

"It's awfully quiet, don't you think?"

"The world... you know..."

"I know..."

"How's quarantine been for you, Vemi?"

"In the future, people will look back and think it was like when tulip bulbs were priced like diamonds or when people thought aeroplanes were angels. It's good we hike out in the fields in broad daylight." Gufo tugged her towards a gap in the hedge between two beech trees. "Let's go in the woods," Vemi said. "No one will see us there for sure."

He decided not to tell her that he had known two people already, one being Nigel from Compliance, who had gone seriously hat-stand-mental from the spores. He decided not to tell her in case this caused one of those rifts between people that could now open if you attempted to explain to someone wrong that they were wrong. He may already be breathing in the spores anyway. The spores disordered your brains. He had reached a point where he didn't care. He hoped his mind would shrug off a spore attack, part reality from any spore-induced illusions like an egg separator splits white from yolk. He no longer cared if his mind was devoured by the fungus from Mars or Metebellis III or wherever it came from. He didn't care while there was a possibility that in some shady glade she would allow him some human moment forbidden by the rules even if this was his last coherent impression of being alive.

They followed Gufo along a tamped-down path towards two more sentry beech trees that aligned with the two back at the hedge. She told him that quarantine had not affected her that much. There were still events to organize. She worked from home, mainly for a discreet agency called Arpeggio. She was in what she described as "the secret events industry." He understood what she meant. As an IT consultant for Celerie Bleu, he always had to keep his clients' intentions private.

The back of her hand brushed the back of his hand.

His head almost exploded.

She told him he looked nice and healthy, big and strong, and asked if he had always looked after himself, always made the effort? He did not know if she was paying him a compliment, or whether she was trying to find out if he had a dodgy past as an alkie, druggie or fat bloke. Out of habit, he nearly blurted his medical history.

He'd realised recently that he was often too eager to give up what as a child had been the distinct or only interesting thing about him. His heart was on the wrong side of his body. This was called dextrocardia. When he'd been a child, he'd pretty much told everyone he met—classmates, playmates, dogs in the street—that he had dextrocardia. He'd got congratulated on being able to pronounce it. As an adult, he felt he needed to admit it straightaway. It was almost like he needed to clear the air or get things straight before anything could proceed.

He was pretty sure now that he should not have explained the heart issue to Mia while they were attacking the free nachos in the VIP gallery bar area fifteen minutes before *Avengers: Age of Ultron* was about to start. He shouldn't have mentioned it to Georgia during the date at the caves, or to Martine in that café on Calico Street because she left five minutes later and she was a doctor, or Miriam on Zoom, or Shannon on Zoom, or Inge on Zoom. He strongly suspected these dalliances had fizzled out because women thought there was something wonky about him, a bit missing.

"I lift weights," he told Vemi. "That's my secret."

"That's your idea of a secret?" she said.

They had arrived at the two beech trees. The tamped-down path continued between them into the woods. Beams of amber sunlight slanted. The world smelled dank. Vemi crouched to let Gufo off his leash. As she leaned over, her hood slipped away from the back of her neck. An exposed strip of skin looked like it wanted to be touched, caressed. It almost hurt that he had no words to ask if she would like this. The no-words were clawing at his face, turning a screw into his face with the long stretches of time between touches, the not-knowing and the dreams within dreams he'd experienced since the Disorder began. Dreams of a ghost with violet eyes. Dreams of the darkness inside a dark building. Dreams in which he was reading a story about someone who entered a dark building and inside found it had no doors or windows, was a room no one sees with no way out. He wasn't even sure this was a dream, that he hadn't read the story after he'd found a battered paperback book abandoned on a seat on a train or a pub bench.

The dog looked up as Vemi unclasped the clip from the collar. Its eyes were huge, more like a man's. It ran up the path and into the woods.

"You OK?" she said.

"Bit weirded out," he said.

"Being outside?"

The woods.

Banks and blankets of drifted leaves.

Secluded shelters hollowed into ancient trunks.

"Being outside," he said.

"Not adventurous, are you?"

"You want me to be?"

She smirked. "Follow Gufo. Gufo knows."

The dog raced ahead until it was a blip squiggling back and forth across the path. From this distance, it looked blue. He wondered if it were some obscure Finnish breed you don't get much over here. He was going to ask her this.

Vemi was meandering slightly ahead of him. The back of her neck was now covered by her hood. How beautiful that hint of the uncovered her had been to him. He ought to tell her. Maybe tell her this instead of telling her that her dog was weird. She obviously loved that dog.

The way the trees formed a tunnel, how they seemed like brassy organ pipes in the orange daylight reminded him of some old-time Walt Disney cartoon and some Saturday morning in the kids' film club, when he'd still been a boy and it was still a long time ago.

○

His mouth felt suddenly dry. Quite a lot of time seemed to have passed in silence. The dog had vanished. In the distance, for a second, the air was thick, like swirling transparent glue. The path ahead widened then pinched, widened then pinched.

He needed an eye test. Only Key Functions were allowed an eye test. He could go blind. No one would care. On the other hand, this could be what it felt like when you breathed in the spores. Maybe these woods were rife with drifting spores.

Vemi had stopped and turned back to face him.

"Someone watches," she said.

Out in the trees stood a woman in a white dress. Her face was a smudge. There was no way of telling how old she was or what sort of state she was in.

"C'mon," he said, "she's probably just doing what we're doing."

"But she's on her own?"

"Not everyone is dead, Vemi, and not everyone is coupled, obviously."

They started along the track again.

"Are you feeling OK?" he said. "She spook you?"

"Seen worse," she said. "When I was at college, we had to cross a park to get to our halls. We stopped doing it on our own because there was a man who would always follow. We called him The Anaesthetist."

"Why?"

"Because one day I was with my friend and he was following us up the path and we had had enough so we turned to confront him, and he was wearing a surgical mask."

"Yikes. What happened?"

"My friend vomited. It grossed him out."

"I mean, was he caught?"

"The Anaesthetist. No one catches The Anaesthetist."

She gave him a funny, eyes-left smile, stopped and in doing so made him stare back. Far back in the distance, the woman in the white dress was standing in the middle of the track.

"I hate her," Vemi said.

Getting spooked out here, that would spoil everything. He tried to lighten things.

"So you and Gufo, you some kind of double act, you finish each other's sentences, read each other's minds?"

"I only read his mind. I not speak dog."

"My cousin's uncle's mum had a black lab that grew to the size of London. It exploded recently."

"What sort of story is that?"

"A true one."

"He lies."

He laughed at the crotchety way she made her voice sound. The air was starting to smell intensely mossy and damp. The treetops swayed. Either side, the beech trees went on and on until they merged with a golden horizon.

Vemi jerked his elbow. "Look."

A second ago, the woman in the white dress hadn't been there. He had scanned in that direction before turning to gaze at the other side. He would have seen her. She was now standing parallel to them, this time close enough to notice her tendrilly mass of tawny hair and that she was barefoot. At this distance, her eyes were a grey blotch. As he tried to focus on them, a terrible sadness fell through him. He wasn't sure why exactly, but somehow he felt he needed a record, evidence, a defence.

He took out his phone.

He took a picture of the woman in the white dress.

"This is now giving me heebies," said Vemi, hurrying him along the track.

"She looks harmless," he said.

"When she moves she moves fast, eh?"

"We were chatting, enjoying ourselves. Maybe we just lost track of time."

He looked back. He couldn't see her.

"These woods have stories," said Vemi.

"I looked up Nether Mundham Woods online yesterday, you know, when you said meet you here. I couldn't find out anything much."

"I didn't think about them until now."

"What stories?"

"It was a long time ago. The seventies."

"What happened?"

"I thought no one comes here ever. You and me could have a quiet time together."

Vemi was jogging along now at a fair clip, gaining a few strides on him.

"Wait," he said. "She's just a girl." He took out his phone and clicked on the photo. He blinked. Blinked again and checked to see if this was the only picture, whether there were more and this one had just come out wrong. Vemi was now leaving him behind. He looked back. About ten meters away, the woman in the white dress was standing in the middle of the path, deep wells of shadow around her eyes, her dress pristine and shapeless, her feet muddy and slick with leaves.

"Hello," he said. "Hello? Can I... can you... go away, please, can you just... fuck the fuck off..."

He turned and sprinted towards Vemi.

"Look." As he paused to get his breath back, he handed her the phone.

Vemi squinted at the screen. "Shit."

"We need to get out of here."

"Which way?"

"Diagonal to the track until we come to the fields."

"What if she's there, too?"

"I don't know," he said. "I don't fancy waiting until dark, do you?"

Vemi turned around in a complete circle and when they were face-to-face again, said, "Gufo. Where is Gufo?"

"He was ahead of us."

"I can't see him."

"We can't leave Gufo here, can we?" he said, not sure whether he was stating the obvious or asking if they could abandon the doggish thing. He craned over her shoulder and stared up the track. No dog. No white dress, either.

"Gufo. What if she has Gufo?" said Vemi, her chin trembling.

"We'll find Gufo," he said. "He can't have gone far."

They walked up the track, calling the dog's name. On either side, the carpet of leaves seemed unusually thick, as if each tree had a superabundance of leaves that when they fell never composted. Leaving the track looked like it meant wading through a shin-deep layer of dead but not decomposing leaves. The stray leaf he picked up from the track was as thick as a pound coin. Looking up, the treetops seemed like they wanted to close over the track. Daylight reached down only through a scar-like slit of pasty sky.

"Gufo!" Vemi called. "Gufo."

"Did you see that?" he said. Out in the trees, a little way back from the path, he was sure he'd seen a grey flicker, a twitch of hind quarters perhaps, or a scrabble of paws. He could easily imagine the dog finding a root or a bone, heaving and gnawing at it out there.

"Do you want me to go and look?"

"Grab his collar. He does not bite."

He glanced at the tree, now unsure he'd seen anything at all now that he was going to have to trudge out there on his own. Beyond the tree, so little, if any light made it through the treetops that it seemed like a starless night had encroached on the middle-distance.

"You'll be OK here?" he said.

"I'll kick her ass if she comes."

"The things I do for you and your dog."

As he trudged into the layer of leaves, flinching as a surge of leaves swamped his trainers, he congratulated himself on the "things I do for you and your dog" line. It was the sort of thing you would say to your girl-friend, when you had history together, but he was saying it after only a few hours. This day would be their bond now, the day they would refer to, in banter, hand-in-hand, side-by-side, forever.

As he approached, there didn't seem to be anything behind the tree. He needed Gufo to be stuck or distracted behind the tree if he were to return to the path with a grin and a dog, if he were to be welcomed back into appreciative arms and a first kiss. He was glad he had not told her about his heart.

He called out the dog's name, hoping it would scoot to his feet. Before the tree, he paused. No rustle. No scuffle. No flutter or birdcall. Beyond: that screen of starless night. A mist of violet flickers hazed across him. He was not sure if they were real floating bits of leaf debris or seeds or spores, or just spangles in his eyes because he was in love again. From behind the tree, a flash of white cotton, a glimpse of muddy foot and bare knee, her eyes, her spiralling violet eyes.

○

"No joy," he said, back on the track with Vemi. He was lying. Joy infused him like sap in a branch. He was so happy he'd met her. He wanted to dance, punch the air, twist the melon, all that. He wanted to stop thinking about whatever he was supposed to be doing and lay back on a hammock made of silk and clouds and picture only her and her lips and thighs and wide eyes and her dreamy, drowsy way of whispering to him.

Vemi turned her back and called out to the trees. "Gufo!... Gooooofoh!"

She hurried ahead. The track was a black slash in a swathe of brown and gold that hung in a circle of night. He was having trouble discerning the difference between the trees now, as if something had coloured in the spaces between the trees. He felt anxious following Vemi up the track, Vemi who called, Vemi who attracted attention to them being together in the woods. This could be misconstrued. She may get jealous and he would have to make it up to her.

○

"What's that?" said Vemi. He'd been pacing behind her through the trees for god knows how long, could have been all night. They had left the path a lifetime ago. She had been shouting, shouting so they would get caught. He had been preoccupied by a dream of indigo dunes and a three-pointed star in the sky and a house where there were rooms beyond rooms and a temple beneath a temple. She was whispering in his ear that there were rooms beyond rooms and a temple beneath the temple where The Compiler would pair and double them. It was hard not to concentrate on the walled building up ahead when she was whispering like this. The whispers dragged on his guts, dragged on his balls. Vemi said, "That's a church."

He would do it in the church.

○

On the graveyard path, Vemi called the dog's name, sometimes through cupped hands, sometimes with her hands wrapped around her chest like she was freezing. The tombstones

were all rounded and caked with moss so green it sometimes looked purple. He meandered through them. Behind him, Vemi shouted. The tombstones leaned. The tombstones slanted. There were scratches on them but he could make out no names or dates. A few had a crude circular pattern gouged into them, perhaps the rings of a tree or a spiral staircase leading down. He knew where Vemi was even though his back was turned and part of him wished to keep it turned and head on through the stones and the trees and into the starless night behind them but he felt her envy, and displeasure when she whispered. Whispered: *fold Vemi in the room no one sees, in places within places and days within days. She knows and dreams, compiles Black Lab, Black Slab, Orange Slab.*

He had his arm around her neck, his other around her waist. She did not scream. He knew that some better part of her wanted him to do this as he pushed her forwards and the great black door of the black flint church loomed and swung open.

○

Inside, the church had a sweetish, rubbish-bin stink that made it hard to breathe. He nudged her forwards. Candles stood in long holders all along the aisle, white ones with an indigo vein in the wax. The flames had a violet tinge that glimmered on the tops of the pews. It was the only church he'd ever visited that didn't have any windows or walls. The nave seemed encased in a rectangle of darkness that reminded him of the low starless night that encircled the woods.

Vemi's shoulders tilted this way and that as she stumbled forward. She was going to say something that was going to make him stop, he hoped. He hated this place but he couldn't hate it. He loved her but he could not love her. He hated her because she hated her.

She disappeared into a bloom of violet light where many, many candles massed at the end of the aisle. As he approached, she was silhouetted against a black oblong slab in front of an arch shape carved into black stone. It was only visible because the groove was filled with a glowing violet substance. On one side, engraved and eight-foot-high was the image of a goddess with an oval aperture in her chest and in the aperture fitted a spiral pattern with an eye at its centre. She opposed another figure of a woman with a cock, or a man with breasts and the head of a stag. Something was arranged on the slab, a pair of wrought-iron shears that rested on thick black twigs set in the same spiral pattern he'd noticed on the tombstones.

From way back came a thud that jumped the base of his spine.

The door to the church had slammed shut.

He had expected the shears to be cold and had prepared himself for a shock when he picked them up. Pleasingly, the handle was warm, moist even. Holding it felt like when you clasp one sweating hand with the other after exercise.

She was staring at her boots. Violet flickers swarmed across her hair and the crown of her head. She had made him do this. She would not let them be happy. She would not let them be together. She had made his choice for him. She was finishing his sentences. He raised the shears level and for the life of him hoped she did not lift her head. If he saw her eyes now, he would let her down, he would fail and become leaves swirling along a tunnel of starless night.

Something shimmered in the violet aura.

Vemi looked up.

The Woman in the White Dress stood beside her.

Violet light whirled across their eyes.

This close up, they looked very similar, sisterish, only one sister had been sleeping rough since a costume party in the seventies where she had come as a wood nymph or Kate Bush or something.

He knew she wanted him to put the shears down, so he put them back where he had found them on the spiral of twigs.

The Woman in the White Dress stood on tiptoes and shimmied her fingers in front of his face like she was trying to swat something from his eyes.

"He is the finest one yet," she said. He could not place her accent. It was a bit singsong-Scandi but not as gentle as Vemi's. It seemed more medieval maiden in a historical drama. "I thank you."

"You say that every time," said Vemi.

"I yearn."

"Yearning ends, you end."

"That is not so."

"It is here."

"I want it to be him. I want to come back to the fireside."

"You brought him here. You could have played with him outside for as long as you liked. I would have returned."

"I want to come inside."

"She knows that," said Vemi. "Not that she knows like we know, or we know like she knows."

She raised her hands and with her fingertips slipped his fleece from his shoulders so it fell to the floor. She reached for the hem of his T-shirt and crept it over his head, threw it aside. Her hands on his chest felt warm, like the shears had felt warm. Her skin felt more like the metal of the shears somehow and not like he had imagined her skin when all he had wanted in the world was to stroke her neck. Now he was standing in front of an altar with strange carvings of distorted animal-monsters, topless in front of two violet ghost-girls when she would be angry with him if he did the wrong thing or chose the wrong one or was chosen by the wrong one. He did not know who he was anymore. The room stank, sweet and fetid. There were black bones in the corners, black bones piled along the rim.

"He has no story," Vemi said. "She likes them like that."

"He fears?"

"She gave him his fear and his fear walked him here."

"He feared solitude?"

"He fears solitude."

Vemi's hand traced an S from his Adam's apple to the centre of his chest. She found a point there and pressed with the heel of her hand.

"Oh," she said. "It's mislaid."

"I am cold," said the Woman in the White Dress.

"She will not shape him."

"But I want to come inside."

"There are more. It's up to her if he gathers now."

"We barter?"

"How?"

"She will listen."

"She is approximate."

They both took a step back and craned their necks, looking at something high up behind him. Vemi dipped her eyes and chin. The Woman in the White Dress appeared on the brink of tears. Her bottom lip trembled. Vemi turned and as she walked back along the aisle, swaying from one side to the other, blew out the candles in the candle holders. Only the vaguest outline of her appeared in the glow shed by the altar candles.

The Woman in the White Dress stood in a semicircle of violet glimmer.

"I love," she whispered.

At her shoulder, Vemi sprang up, face pinched, stern as she spun the Woman in the White Dress around by her elbow. As her back turned to him for the first time, she was hollow. No dress, no skin, no spine, no blood-red insides, only a chamber like the interior of a dead tree trunk that shimmered and swirled before she vanished.

All the candles around the altar snuffed.

Darkness engulfed.

Out in the darkness, a heavy door slammed.

He remembered who he was. He was looking for a dog. His heart was in the wrong place. He should have said. Something behind him twitched, something bulky enough to unsettle the air. At his shoulder now, something wanted. Something wanted what was left.

THE OUTER DARK
PODCAST & SYMPOSIUM

Our mission is to foster conversation and connect communities among the diverse slate of creators and audience members under the umbrella of speculative fiction - inclusive, safe and welcoming to women, LBGTQIA+, and writers of color.

THE WEIRD IS ALWAYS UNEXPECTED
EXPECT THE UNEXPECTED IN 2022

For the latest details, keep in touch

LISTEN ON THIS IS HORROR
TWITTER @THEOUTERDARK
THEOUTERDARK.ORG

Sunder Island

ĜƉ

Derrick Boden

"A moderately bad man knows he is not very good: a thoroughly bad man thinks he is all right." —C.S. Lewis

Smith-Jansen Meteorological Station incident report, exhibit A: twenty-eight handwritten pages from the personal journal of Company Inspector B-12462, Ellen Rodriguez (psych profile unavailable), recovered thirty-five nautical miles east-northeast of Paraskuntakeet Island.

Monday, September 1
3 p.m.

The coastline was a balled fist of rock jutting through the fog, bird shit sprayed like cancer spots across its knuckles. The captain of the *Merry Mae*, a bitter man named Mr. Yamamoto who hadn't shaved since sometime in his early childhood, reassured me that it was a clear day by Paraskuntakeet standards. He said the shoals bring the fog. Like I gave a shit. Yamamoto hadn't said a word to me the entire eight-day voyage from Perth. Something about women and bad luck at sea. Now we were finally here, and he was getting all sentimental.

"Be on the dock Friday morning, *madam*." He leered at me with jaundiced eyes. "Or we leave without you."

The dock in question was long, crooked, half-rotten. My company shirt was already soaked heavy from the damp air. I shouldered past the captain's extended hand, flung my duffel onto the dock and disembarked.

Yamamoto leaned over the bulwark, whispered a hurried warning into my ear. His breath stank of pickled fish but his words chilled me to the marrow.

I jammed a cigarette between my numb lips and made for shore. The last thing I need is another man who knows what's best for me. Besides, I didn't come all this way to turn back. The company is paying me to track down Francis Turner, and goddammit I'm going to find him.

I could feel Yamamoto's eyes on me all the way to the base of the dock, where patches of sickly brown scrub clung to an embankment. Nearby, someone had stacked a pile of bones on a patch of red-stained dirt. They could've been chicken bones, if chickens grew waist-high. The bones were gnawed and gristly.

The weather thinned. I caught a glimpse of a man standing at the top of the hill, looking down. Baby blue polo, spotless khakis, a flash of teeth. Then the fog thickened again, and he was gone. I rooted through my duffel, found the utility knife they told me I wouldn't need. Jammed it into my belt. It didn't make me feel any safer.

A low horn announced the *Merry Mae*'s departure, beginning its five-night circuit of the neighboring islands.

I was alone.

9 p.m.

The Smith-Jansen Meteorological Station clings to the hilltop like an aluminum barnacle, like a crusty metal spore pod waiting to burst. It's a Cold War relic, important enough to keep the lights on but not enough to bankroll its staff. All that's left of the old eight-person crew is a pair of live-in contractors that share a paycheck. The company sends an inspector out twice a year to copy data onto a thumb drive, document any equipment failures, report back.

The last inspector never reported back.

By the time I crested the hill for the first time, mud had wormed its way into my boots, between my toes. I was soaked through to my bra, shivering and miserable. Ominous as it was with its jutting vanes and its panels peeling like leper-flesh, the station was a welcome sight.

The sentiment didn't last.

Gouges ran the width of the metal door. Deep, ragged cuts from some kind of weapon, or the claws of a beast. A few feet away sat another cairn of grisly bones.

The door swung open on well-oiled hinges. The lights flickered on without a fuss. At a glance, everything looked in order: pristine floors, rain slicks hanging in a row, daily check-list printed on company letterhead. But I could already tell something was wrong. For starters, the place was deserted.

According to the company, the station is the only modern structure on the island. But given the unplugged fridge and the stripped beds, nobody had overnighted in some time. The whole place reeked of bleach. Even with the lights on, shadows converged in the corners of the observatory, the back of the server room, the ends of every hall. The metal walls offered little warmth.

The daily checklist seemed straightforward enough: swap out the solar batteries, cycle the rainwater tanks, transcribe anything notable from the meteorological equipment. A column labeled "tend the goats" had been scratched out. The last entry read September 1. Today.

The signature to the right of each entry said, simply, *Andre*. Something about its bold, crisp letters set my teeth on edge.

By the time I'd scoped out the place, it was almost dark. I found some old bedding in storage, shook off a few years of dust, set up a bunk at the better-lit end of the dorms. My limbs were like bags of lead, even though all I'd done for a week is pace the length of the *Merry Mae* and try not to think about Jerome, swinging from our garage rafters by his favorite tie.

I stepped outside for a smoke. Halfway down the inland slope, a man limped around a clearing outside a corrugated aluminum hut. It wasn't the same man I'd seen earlier—this guy was shorter, stooped, frail. He wore a pair of moccasins and a tweed bathrobe. I could see the gray curls of his chest hair poking through from here. He didn't see me, and something about his scowl made me glad for it.

Across the hillside, ragged red birds clawed out from thatch nests, shook dirt clods from their wings, scrabbled at the soggy earth. One of them staggered up to the station, not ten paces away. It was twice the size of a goose, and judging by its shitty wings, flightless. Vicious claws, wicked hooked beak. It watched me with human eyes.

I crushed my cigarette on the station door, locked myself inside, dug out my journal. I'd better keep a record of what happens here.

Tomorrow I'll track down Francis Turner.

I smoked three cigarettes thinking it over. Halfway through the third, the man in the polo emerged through the fog. He navigated the hillside like a gazelle. There was nowhere else he could be going but here.

○

Here's what Yamamoto said at the dock.

He said the people on this island, they're not of this earth.

There was a shipwreck, some years back. Whalers, real rugged men. According to Yamamoto, the islanders—European emigrants, he said; the island had no indigenous population—murdered every last one of the whalers. Strapped them to spits, roasted them, fed their meat to the birds. Used their bones as windchimes, their flesh for clothing.

He said this is no place for a woman. I decided not to point out that the shipwrecked crew were all men, and look how much good that did them.

It was probably bullshit, anyhow. The company assured me the island is uninhabited aside from the two contractors (whose names they promised to provide, but never did), and hopefully Francis Turner. Still, Yamamoto's story stuck with me.

Rumors always come from somewhere.

Tuesday, September 2
8:30 a.m.

Slept like shit. The peroxide stench was nauseating, and the wind battered the metal walls all night long. Sometime after midnight, I'd had enough. I salvaged a tent from storage, pitched it outside, caught a few hours of sleep. Dawn came too early and too bright, even through the mist. I scoured the kitchen for provisions.

Bad news: no coffee. Should've brought my own.

Worse: I'm missing four packs of cigarettes. Only two packs left. Gotta start rationing.

1 p.m.

The man in the polo's name is Andre, but he kept calling himself *the patient*. He's tall and well-built and his smile is the warmest thing I've seen on Paraskuntakeet. But there's something unsettling in the shift of his eyes.

He told me he lives in the hut with the other man, the one with the limp. Called him *the doctor*.

I asked him what kind of doctor, and if he was still practicing.

Andre frowned politely. "The doctor has helped me in so very many ways, Inspector. He is a good man."

I glanced downhill. The doctor was out again, flinging bird shit from the clearing with a shovel in short, angry strokes. His scowl was, if anything, deeper.

"Sure." I thought about the two men living in that cramped hut for all this time. I thought about the signature on the station checklist. "What made you take this job, way out here?"

He smiled. "What made you take this job, way out here?"

I was about to tell him it wasn't remotely the same, I'd be gone by Friday, when the glint in his eye drove a chill through my body. He wasn't asking to make a point, I realized, and he was gleaning an answer from my silence even now.

The truth: I'm here to escape. To create distance from the judging eyes and the groping hands. I'm here to prove Jerome wrong, that I can in fact finish something I've started. I'm here because if I had stayed one day longer, I might have ended up like him.

I shrugged. "Where's Francis Turner?"

A blank smile.

"The last inspector. Company never got his report. It's been six months."

His smile persisted. "Are you unwell, Inspector?"

I fought the urge to reach for the knife at my belt. "I'm fine."

"Would you like some narcotics?"

"Excuse me?"

"Gutsalve. It's quite relaxing, and completely harmless."

I've been sober for eight months. Might as well have been eight hours. "I don't think so."

"Suit yourself."

"I will."

"Do let me know if there's any way I can make your stay more pleasant, Inspector."

I watched him maneuver downhill to the hut, where the doctor shook his fist at him and muttered angry words I couldn't hear. He put his hands on Andre's shoulders, forced him to a knee, tilted his head back. He withdrew a small bottle from the pocket of his bathrobe, held it to each of Andre's eyes in turn.

Andre departed without a word.

6:30 p.m.

The doctor was shooing a flightless bird from his porch with a rolled-up shirt when I reached the hut. I could just make out the company logo and embroidered name—DR WELLS—on the shirt's breast as he cracked it against the bird's shabby tail feathers.

"Thought they were nocturnal," I said.

"Red rails never sleep." He eyed me with contempt. "Vile creatures."

"I'm Ellen Rodriguez, from—"

"I don't like unexpected guests."

"They didn't tell you I was coming?"

"How would they?"

It was a fair point, though it raised more questions than it answered. For instance. "How do they even pay you?"

The doctor raised an eyebrow.

Could these people not answer a single question?

"The company. How do you get your paycheck for this shit job?"

"Direct deposit."

I wasn't sure if it was meant to be a joke.

The bird had taken advantage of the doctor's distraction and maneuvered between him and the hut. Presently, it lunged for the entrance.

The doctor whirled. *Crack* went the shirt. Blood spattered the corrugated siding. A single feather dislodged, landed in the mud. The bird retreated behind a shrub.

I couldn't un-see the look in the creature's eyes. Still can't.

I didn't know birds could weep.

The doctor scowled. "Are we done, Inspector?"

"I met your friend Andre."

"That man is not my friend."

"Doesn't he live—"

"He is a wicked man."

I watched the shirt in his hand, slowly spinning. Primed. I wondered what it would take for him to turn it on me.

I decided to find out.

"Was Francis Turner a wicked man, too?"

"Get off my porch."

"What happened to him, doctor?" I narrowed my eyes. "What did you do?"

The bird darted around the shrub, snatched its lost feather from the porch and retreated. The sun slipped behind the gauzy fog bank. Across the hillside, more birds pried themselves from their nests. A small posse of them converged on their injured kin, harassed it with side-jabs that drew more blood and loosed the feather from its beak. The posse tore the feather to shreds.

The doctor showed me his back. "Enjoy your stay, Inspector."

10:30 p.m.

Tonight I watched a flightless bird pick apart the carcass of one of its own. The dissection was ruthless, surgical. It pried feathers from skin, bones from flesh, *pop pop pop*. It sucked down the entrails like earthworms. It savored the eyes.

The doctor called them red rails, but I know that's bullshit. Jerome had been a birder, which meant by our third anniversary my head was full of bird trivia. Red rails were indeed flightless island birds. But they've been extinct for a few hundred years.

And I doubt they were cannibals.

I sucked down the day's last cigarette, tried not to think of how few I had left. Through the thinning mist, I spotted movement. Something large, lithe, fleet.

I ducked behind a shrub, peered through its anemic leaves.

It was Andre. Some hundred feet away, prowling the hillside on all fours. The sleeves of his polo were rolled all the way up; his pale skin glistened in the moonlight. Mud caked his bare hands and feet.

The hell was he doing? Foraging? Hunting? Spying?

I remembered his words—*are you unwell, Inspector?*—and retreated into my tent, my memory, my regret. If I thought I'd find peace out here, I couldn't have been more wrong. This place makes me feel separated. Like someone is grabbing my left ear, and someone else my right, and they're slowly pulling me in two.

9 a.m.

I'm out of smokes. I swear I had a pack left when I zipped myself into my tent for the night. But I've turned the whole goddamn thing inside out, and my smokes are gone.

The thought of forty-eight hours without a cigarette makes me want to pry out my eyes. It also gives me a jolt of urgency. I'm halfway through my stay on this godforsaken island, and I'm still no closer to finding Francis Turner.

If the doctor and his patient won't cooperate, I'll have to root him out myself.

12 p.m.

Nothing ever dries on Paraskuntakeet. I've stopped noticing the condensation that gathers on my eyebrows and saturates my hair, but I'll never get used to damp socks. My feet are cold and wilted. I think a lot about ringworm and gangrene.

The north coast is an absolute bog. I nearly lost a boot to the muck during my futile attempt at mapping the island. A pair of red rails watched with beady eyes as I flailed against the mud-grip, as if waiting to close in and feast on my flesh.

I untied my laces and slipped free. I was retrieving my boot with a stick when the temperature dropped a few degrees. I glanced up.

"May I offer some assistance?"

Andre was a blurry silhouette against the mist. Today his polo was salmon. His smile was as pleasant as ever.

I remembered what the doctor had said about him. "No thanks."

In fact, I was a mess. I could hardly get my boot back on my own foot, what with the tremble of my fingers from the nicotine withdrawal. My legs were mud-spattered past the knee.

"Suit yourself."

He made no move to leave.

My hand drifted to my belt. My knife wasn't there. Where had I left it?

"I found a well along the coast," I said. "A few caves, some old tools."

"You are thorough, Inspector."

It was a strange thing to say. The caves were easy to spot from a hundred paces. "What happened to them?"

"Ma'am?"

"The people that lived here before."

"Ah, yes."

He glanced out to sea, said nothing more.

"Who were they?"

"They were Dutch."

"Colonists?" I hesitated. "Shipwreck survivors?"

He shrugged. "I cannot say."

"Meaning you don't know, or—"

"I can only speak of their time on the island." His smile faded a little. "They suffered a rash of stillbirths. One after another, for years. They began performing rituals—second baptisms, blood rites. They ingested large doses of gutsalve, slept on their hands. Nothing worked."

He let out a perfunctory sigh. "A group threw themselves from the cliffs on Christmas Day. The rest followed in short order. They solved their problem of birth with death."

"Where are they buried?"

He glanced inland. A clutch of red rails fought over something thin and white.

When he looked back, his smile had vanished. "The doctor says the island takes us apart."

"Is that what happened to Francis Turner?"

"He was not a good person, Inspector."

Was. "Where is he?"

No response.

"What about me? Am I a good person?"

The cordial smile returned. "Why, Inspector. We've only just met."

One of the rails made off with the white object clutched in its beak.

It was a bone.

10:30 p.m.

This gutsalve shit is no joke.

I knocked on the hut door with a tight-balled fist, bang bang bang. It was sometime after dusk. I think. Time has been a slinky tonight. Could've been mid-afternoon. Hell, maybe it all happened to someone else.

The doctor grudgingly invited me in.

The place was small, stale, cramped. Whole goddamn island to spread out on, and they live in a skanky one-room tin can. I'll never understand men.

Old TV in the corner, DVDs stacked on top. Dented kettle on a bachelor range. Pinup on the wall adjacent the bunks. Very dated, very raunchy.

I asked the doctor some questions. Damned if I can remember his answers.

Something I said must've loosened him up, though, because all of a sudden he offered some gutsalve. My hands were shaking, no coffee all week, no smokes all day, not sleeping for shit, Jerome hanging from the rafters, his legs swinging bang bang bang against the Civic, and I thought... what the hell.

Turns out those ugly brown shrubs I've been seeing, that's gutsalve. You chew the leaves like coca. Tastes like a lukewarm shot of Jäger. I didn't vomit, at least.

Nothing happened. Maybe I'm immune, I said. Doc said just wait.

I said, "What happened to the goats?"

"Excuse me?"

"The station checklist mentioned goats."

"Oh, those." As if there'd been others. "We ate them."

I coughed up a stem.

"Eventually one tires of sardines and potatoes."

Banggg.

Doc said, working now?

Yep.

I glanced around the room, chasing watercolor trails. I noticed things. A mound of red feathers, globbed in some kind of resin. Or dried blood. A needle, a lighter, a bottle of India ink.

Five crumpled packs of smokes, same brand as mine.

"Where's Francis Turner?"

"I have no idea."

"Your patient says he's a bad dude."

"I would not trust that man."

"Which one?"

He did not elaborate.

"Is Turner still on the island?"

He held his hand out, palm down. Tilted it side to side.

○

Jerome's brother Vincent came to my room at the summer lodge the night before our third anniversary. Jerome was in town restocking the firewood. We'd been fighting all vacation. Little things—thermostat battles, hair in the shower drain. The top two buttons of Vincent's shirt were open. He smelled like campfire and rum.

The wicked part of me says, see? Vincent came to me. I never would've gone to him. And there was also the rum.

The other part of me—the guilty part—calls bullshit. I was wearing a bathrobe. Could've pulled on some pants before answering the door, instead of hitting my collar with a shot of perfume. Could've turned him away.

Regardless, it happened.

When things go south, we compartmentalize.

We wake up, think: oh, Jesus. Not again. Then we think: that isn't really me. Or: that is me, but I can change. I'll be a better person, starting today. Right now. We take a hot shower, too hot, scrub the offending scent from our body, shave twice until we're raw and maybe a little bloody.

We open our journal, make a list of the things we hate about ourselves. We resolve to overcome them all at once. We'll start complimenting people. We'll leave bigger tips. We won't argue with our partner about stupid shit. We'll call our mother, put some serious thought into our career, go back to school. We'll definitely start working out, jogging or at least walking more. Five thousand steps a day. Call it three thousand.

And maybe it works, for a day. Maybe a week, if we're feeling it. Then we slip.

We always slip.

So we tear out the page, find a new one, make a new list. There are so many pages torn out already, but this time it'll be different.

And so on.

Until the day we walk into the garage with an awkward armload of laundry, mumbling to ourselves to just buy a goddamn hamper already, and we find that our husband has hanged himself with a strip of paisley formal attire.

There are not enough blank pages in the journal to fill our list that day, or any day thereafter.

Thursday, September 4
8:30 a.m.

Gutsalve keeps you awake, but not alert. Or maybe that's just the island. Outside fog, inside fog.

I woke early to find a pile of bird bones and gristle outside my tent. I left it untouched, went directly to the nearest shrub. Chew chew chew.

Banggg.

One day left. Still no leads. I'm running out

of time.

I scoured the station. Front to back, inside out. A ship had dropped Turner off six months ago. In all likelihood, he'd gone straight to the station, just like me. Checked the incident report, counted the wet cells, downloaded the weather data.

But then what?

I rifled through storage. Checked under every bunk. Turned the rain slicks inside out.

Nothing.

I wandered into the kitchen. The panoramic window would've made it a great lookout spot, if the whole station wasn't wrapped in fog. I leaned over the sink, peered into the mist. Some hundred paces away, a light flicked on, then off again. I leaned closer, squinted—

A coastal gust sent the metal walls rattling. I leapt backward, slammed into the pantry. The door popped open, revealing a neat row of canned soup. All cream of mushroom, all expired. I'd seen it already, nothing new. What I hadn't noticed was the scrap of paper in the back, half-hidden by the cans. I reached in, grabbed it. It was a handwritten note.

I read it.

Then I turned and ran.

○

I found Andre at the dock. He stood peering over his sneakers into the water. The edges of his body looked frayed, like he was coming apart at the seams. Or maybe that was the gutsalve playing tricks on my eyes.

I stopped ten paces away, said: "Doctor."

He didn't look up. "I'm sorry, Inspector. I believe you're mistaking me for someone else."

"I saw—" I stopped myself, started over. "Tell me your full name."

The tide slapped at the rotting pylons, sucked silt from the shallows, slapped again.

Finally, he glanced up. Smiled warmly. "Just Andre."

"Come on, man. I don't have time for this—"

"Earlier, you asked why I enjoy living here."

He spread his arms. "On the island, I can have just one name."

Very spiritual. Also bullshit. "I found a note in the station. Something about rations, lactose intolerance. It was signed by you."

"And?"

"It said *Dr. Andre Wells.*"

He kept looking at me, arms spread, smile unwavering.

I stifled the urge to retreat.

"You're him," I said. "Or he's you."

It was a weird thing to say. How could one person have two bodies? I'd seen them together, doctor and patient. Good, and wicked.

And yet.

"Like yourself, Inspector?"

"There's only one of me."

He cocked his head. "Then who wanders the hills at night with your eyes attached?"

Banggg.

Friday, September 5
12:30 a.m.

It's past midnight as I write this, the last night of my stay. Yamamoto will be here at dawn. I'm sitting in the dark outside my tent, waiting for Andre. It isn't me that wanders the hills at night, and I'm going to prove it. By the tightness in my throat and the sweat on my frigid brow, I know he'll show.

This time, I'll be ready.

I've been chewing gutsalve to stay awake. The fog has slipped into my ears. I'm looking down at my mud-caked boots and my frayed edges, and I'm wondering: *why did I come here?*

It doesn't matter. Tonight is my last chance to find Francis Turner. I'm not going back without—

There. Beneath the rising mist, fifty paces downhill. A flash of pale skin, pale eyes, pale teeth.

Andre, the patient, prowls the hillside like a feral cat. Hunting.

I'm going after him.

9 a.m.

I am alive. Steeped in blood, wrists lacerated, reeking. But alive. I'd better write this down quickly, before my memories dissolve into fog. Here's what happened:

I followed Andre down the slope, into the southern valley where rocks jut from the mud like teeth through rotting gums. He stalked on all fours, leaping across gorges and scuttling downhill. He moved with the agility of an ibex, the silence of a wraith.

I trailed as far back as I could without losing sight of him. But I was clumsy in the mud, and as the terrain steepened I stumbled into a gutsalve thicket. Branches snapped.

Andre froze, sniffed the air, glanced back.

I flattened myself against the ground, pressed my cheek to the muck. My heart pounded against my ribcage, against the cold mud, into the bones of the island and straight up Andre's own legs no doubt.

But when I gathered the courage to glance up, he was already crawling deeper into the mist. I hastened after him, all the way to the southern coast where the Indian Ocean gorged itself on the shoreline in slow, noisy bites.

It was here that Andre caught his prey.

His movements were economical, vicious. Lunge, twist, snap, shred. The red rail never saw him coming. Its eyes bulged in shock even as its blood sprayed the nearby rocks.

I thought about the bone piles scattered across the island. I thought about the colonists. The shipwreck survivors. Francis Turner.

Andre laid the bird face-up on a boulder. He probed it with his fingers, then dug into the flesh on either side of its keel. *Pop* went the bone from the gristle. Blood drizzled along his forearms.

He unrolled a plastic bag, dropped the keel bone inside.

Next he spread the chest cavity and extracted the entrails. I remembered the cannibal bird from my second night here, wondered if Andre would suck down the viscera just the same.

Instead, he deposited the mass into his bag.

Next came the feathers, pluck pluck pluck. Then with a twist and a jerk, the beak.

When he reached for the eyes, I had to look away.

Mistake.

I glanced back, and he was gone. I sat bolt upright, squinted into the thickening mist. Had I made a noise? Had he known I was here all along?

I turned to run, but it was too late. There he was, looming over me, fingers wrapped around my forearm.

On his lips, so very close, was no trace of a smile.

○

Andre didn't utter a word the whole way back to the hut. He dragged me through the mud, across the rocks. My instinct was to fight back, but the hardness of his glare told me that would be a terrible mistake. All I could do was stagger along to keep from falling.

Outside the hut he lashed my wrists with hemp, staked me to the ground, then went inside.

The fog was mud-thick. I couldn't see past the ragged edges of the clearing. I thought about Yamamoto's warning, wondered what my bones would sound like rattling in the coastal breeze. I wondered if he'd kill me before extracting them.

The *Merry Mae* was due at dawn. If I didn't reach the dock in time, they'd leave without me. The only thing worse than being killed tonight was being kept alive, here, with them.

With myself. With Jerome, feet swinging from the rafters of my skull. With Vincent, his hand on my shoulder at the funeral, his brother not three days cold. And my hand on his.

The fog in my brain was thinning, and I didn't like what I saw. This wasn't about Francis Turner. Maybe he'd left long ago, maybe he was dead, maybe both. It made no difference. This was about me, now.

I spotted a gutsalve shrub at the edge of the clearing, strained against my bonds to reach it. The hemp dug into my wrists, drew blood.

The pain brought clarity. What a fool I was, ready to saw my own hands off for one last hit of psychotropics. I was still alive. There was still hope.

From the hut came noises. Two voices raised in disagreement. An arrhythmic hiss, like water drops on a hot griddle. The snap of fabric against flesh.

I pried at my cuffs, only succeeded at tightening them against my bloody wrists. A cry escaped my lips.

The hut fell silent.

I clamped my mouth shut.

The door swung open. A man stepped out. It took me a minute to realize it was Andre.

He was shirtless. Tattoos covered his chest and back—scrawled words, a rambling list of misconduct. *Bites nails. Leaves hair in the drain. Spies on the neighbors. Disembowels vagrants under the interstate; photographs the life vacating their eyes.* And so on.

Andre's body was a confession.

Then there was the rest of him. Every piece of the dissected red rail from the southern coast had been attached to his body. Leather straps bound the bird's keel to his sternum. Feathers clumped in blood bristled down his arms and back. Talons extended from his fingers. Its beak elongated the ridge of his own nose.

He approached in swift lunges. Loomed over me, spread his feathered arms.

When I looked into his eyes, I saw Jerome.

Banging against the hood of the Civic. And before that.

Fucking in the back seat, while he thought I was across town. Evelyn. Saya. The girl from the pool hall with the tight ass. My bridesmaid Yvonne.

Jerome's eyes narrowed. He drove his heels into the earth, raised his claws above his head, raked them down, down, down.

○

The next time I blinked, the fog was paling from the onset of dawn. The world was a dull gray. My wrists were still bound; my shirt was torn. I was covered in blood, mine or the bird's or both. My body was numb.

Sitting next to me: the doctor.

He avoided eye contact. "This is unfortunate."

"Fuck you."

He winced, managed to recover into a sneer.

"If you feel so bad," I said. "Let me go."

"He'll be back any moment."

I tried not to imagine what Andre had in store for me.

In the distance, muted by the fog: a horn.

The *Merry Mae*.

I was too late. The hill would block my screams for help, and for what? To drag Yamamoto's men into this circle of death? They're sailors, not soldiers. They wouldn't stand a chance.

The doctor glanced over his shoulder. In his eyes, a flicker of terror. Andre was coming.

"Who is he?" I asked. What I meant was, *who are you?*

"A wicked man. I warned you."

"Answer my question."

Another furtive glance. "There comes a time when we simply cannot live with ourselves any longer. Isn't that right, Inspector?"

I said nothing. Across the clearing, a red rail skulked.

"We wear masks." He stared at his hands. "We push ourselves out. Through our pores, into the mist."

The bird stared at me with guilty eyes.

Were they mine?

I remembered the Civic. The women. The excuses I made for him, for us.

After his death, that other part of me—the guilty part—had packed it all away. Shouldered the blame. Now, somehow, that part of me was gone. Pushed out.

A shout carried from uphill. Gruff, unfamiliar. Naive.

Yamamoto had sent one of his men to look for me.

He'd be dead the second he set foot in this clearing. I clamped my mouth shut, shrunk into silence. My only hope was that he'd pass me by, return empty-handed but alive.

No such luck. The heavyset man materialized through the fog, spotted me, picked up his pace. The doctor had already slunk back to his hut; his patient was almost here. I shouted a warning, then a plea. Turn back. *Get to the fucking ship.*

He didn't hear me, or didn't listen either way. He just kept coming, long arrogant strides down the hill, a foolish lumbering knight. He reached the clearing, severed my bonds.

I shouted *run* but it was already too late. Andre was there, clawed and beaked. The blood spattered my face, then my back as I fled uphill. There was no scream—just the wet hacking of meat. I ran all the way to the top, past the station, down the other side to the dock where the *Merry Mae* lurked, half-consumed in fog off shore.

A pontoon thumped against the dock's pylon. I boarded, untied the rope, yanked at the engine's choke. I didn't look back.

○

The crew wanted to storm the island, squeeze revenge from its soggy flesh. They brandished knives, crowbars, a rusted machete. It nearly came to mutiny, but Yamamoto held firm. The captain wanted nothing to do with this place, could not leave its shoals fast enough. His man had acted alone in coming to shore, and by the captain's decree any who followed would be left behind.

For once, I agreed with him. I placed a bloodied hand on his shoulder and said, *this is no place for a man.*

I'll wait until tomorrow to tell him the rest—that I've no intention of returning to Perth, that I have no report to give and that the company can go to hell. I'm already regretting this journal, and I'm sure I'll throw these pages overboard by week's end.

I am certain none of this will surprise Yamamoto. I'm not the first inspector he's brought to Paraskuntakeet, after all—though once he submits his own report, I might be the last.

We leave the island as we came upon it: entombed in fog. I'm huddled at the ship's stern under a scratchy blanket, watching the mist dissolve the station, the shoreline, the pier. Before the last pylon vanishes into memory, I catch sight of two figures at the end of the dock. One is hobbled by a bum leg; the other kneels obediently, head tilted back. The man with the limp squirts serum into the other man's eyes.

The doctor, forever tinkering with his patient.

The island takes us apart, he'd said. What I didn't know at the time was that this is exactly what the doctor wanted.

Just like me. And perhaps not unlike the doctor, with that guilt-stricken part of myself left haunting the Paraskuntakeet fog, I'm not sure what's left of me.

As I watch, the doctor withdraws a journal from his bathrobe, jots a hasty note. Making a list of the things he hates about himself. Resolving to overcome them all.

This time, I can almost hear him think, *it'll be different.*

Being an Anthology of Original Weird Fiction

LOOMING LOW

VOLUME II

Edited by Justin Steele and Sam Cowan

Cover art: Yves Tourigny

22 BRAND NEW TALES OF WONDER AND HORROR FROM SOME OF TODAY'S BEST PRACTITIONERS OF THE WEIRD:

Matthew M. Bartlett
Nadia Bulkin
Brian Evenson
Kurt Fawver
Gemma Files
Richard Gavin
Craig Laurance Gidney
Cody Goodfellow
Michael Griffin
Michael Kelly
Gwendolyn Kiste
Anya Martin
S.P. Miskowski
David Peak
Erica Ruppert
Clint Smith
Simon Strantzas
Jeffrey Thomas
Brooke Warra
Kaaron Warren
A.C. Wise
Alvaro Zinos-Amaro

LOOMING LOW VOLUME II is the follow-up anthology to the award-winning *Looming Low Volume I* (2017). Lead Editor Justin Steele (*The Children of Old Leech, Strange Aeons*) and fourteen authors are back from *Volume I* alongside eight authors new to the series. *Looming Low Volume II* will be available in deluxe limited hardcover, trade paperback, and e-book editions. Coming Fall 2022.

For more information or to be added to the mailing list, visit dimshores.com.

DIM SHORES

Post Office Box 3092
Citrus Heights, CA
95611-3092, USA
DIMSHORES.COM

FIGMENTS OF THE NIGHT

ARMEL DAGORN

The straw boys arrived when everyone was already a few drinks in. Oonagh hadn't thought about it, the possibility of them coming, but now they were here, in their ample work-worn clothes, the straw cones over their heads like they'd got stuck in a vase. And it made perfect sense, after other weddings she'd been to or heard about, that they'd come for her too.

A few people cheered as the straw boys entered, and most smiled, as if relieved for the new attraction, for the interruption of struggling conversations, the temporary respite from having to keep up the merriment.

Oonagh saw her mother tense, thinking no doubt of the buffet, and the crates of stout she'd taken in case, as a reserve, and that Joe Spillane had agreed to take back if the guests' thirst didn't reach that far. Oonagh spotted Claire by the buffet. She rose from the table to go to her friend. The three figures unsettled her, with their inhuman pointed heads, the walls of straw where faces should have been. The musicians had paused when the straw boys had entered, just an instant, a missed heartbeat, but now they'd got themselves and their riffs back together. The dancers flung their feet around again, no longer looking at each other but instead at the three figures that had stomped into their midst and that now grossly imitated their moves, throwing their limbs exaggeratedly, like dolls play-acting some child's vision of a ballroom. Oonagh knew the straw boys would get to her eventually, would have to come congratulate or tease the bride, but her instinct was still to try and avoid them.

"Give us drink!" shouted one of the straw boys, the heaviest one, from the bench he'd climbed on. "Drink for good fortune, how's that? Drink's a cheap price!"

"Better give them, now," Claire said, and Oonagh just nodded. Her mother was already crossing the dance floor with three opened bottles of stout, the two in her right hand hanging by their necks from the hooks of her fingers, the third in her left hand held tightly like something that might try to escape.

It was obviously Tadhg O'Shea, that strong straw boy. The hard voice, the rough swing of his shoulders as he walked across fields, now further amplified by drinks. She knew they'd probably have had a drink before setting off. They'd have made the most of their outfits, no doubt walking with their straw heads on, choosing a path by friendly houses where they knew a drink could be had without too much coaxing.

Oonagh had been four or five when she'd seen her father getting ready in the bedroom, sitting on his bed with old clothes on, one of her mother's skirts on over pants. She'd stood in the dark, staring in as he picked up the tall straw cone and lifted it to bring down over his head.

She hadn't understood then, but for years after that she'd felt a certain unease at times with her father, even though he'd grown old and frail before he died. This sense of menace still lingered in her memory, whenever she thought of him. It was the strangest thing, that a man could become another, simply by donning a cone of straw.

The straw boys took the bottles Oonagh's mother handed them. O'Shea had come down from the bench, and he bowed exaggeratedly at her back. He raised the bottle high and shouted, "To the bride!" The second straw boy lifted his too, but the third just stood there bottle in hand, swaying like a reed in a soft breeze. The toast was echoed shyly here and there around the room, and Oonagh was happy when the hum of conversation resumed and she wasn't the centre of attention anymore.

She couldn't take her eyes off the men, though. O'Shea brought his free hand to his straw cone, and, pushing open the stalks with two fingers in a V, made a red, wet mouth appear, and brought his bottle to it. Oonagh felt he was staring at her, with those vile lips of his,

even though she couldn't see anything but the faceless straw.

For a while Oonagh thought she might be fine. O'Shea took up with a group of men in a corner of the room, and stood there bantering, a hand in his pocket and another on a bottle, as if he were really a man and not a straw-crowned creature that had snuck in from the night. As they didn't show any signs of wanting to approach her, Oonagh relaxed, went from friend to friend, from cousin to brother, enjoyed their good will and drunken glee. By her third bottle of stout she felt light-headed, but it was supposed to be good for her. All that iron.

She slipped outside when she managed to escape her well-wishers. The cold air came as a relief, piercing through the sweat on every inch of her skin. She walked from the building, past the bicycles piled against the dry-stone wall, the few cars. She stopped when the light from the open door at her back did not reach her anymore, when the noise from the inside revelling became just a little distant, and turned around. She saw the village hall sitting there among the fields, and in her mind it was a cube of light, a bright tank of revelling, of drunk twirling and dropping things. The dark, thick walls of the hall were the night putting a lid on it, tolerating their desperate human feast, as long as it remained caged in. As if the night let them be, or, perhaps, as if they were nothing but figments of the night's imagination. Her fellow villagers in there, fighting against the eternal hurtling through the night. And she felt herself side with it. With the dark fields and the stone walls racing through them like scabies. Siding with the night, despite the things that roamed it.

A shape darkened the doorway. For an instant it stood there, swaying, its straw hat pointing up, and Oonagh froze, thinking the straw boy had come for her. He stumbled forward then, lifting the cone off his head, and bent in two, as if punched in the stomach by an unseen presence. He threw up, and when he straightened up between spurts Oonagh recognised him. Tom O'Neill. His boyish cheeks shiny in moonlight. She almost laughed, seeing such a soft boy in the straw outfit. That she'd been scared of this.

There'd been a time, the previous summer, when she'd fantasised about a married life with Tom. It had only lasted a few weeks, but in those days, when he was back from the town where he trained as a mechanic, he helped his father in the fields, and not many days ever passed that she didn't come across him as she walked to and from the shop. She came to wonder if he arranged for them to meet so, if he came out when she was due out of work, and hung around crossroads with his cows, letting them linger there according to their lazy nature, grazing the muddy roadside grass. Tinkered with posts and fences along her homeward route, finding tiny flaws that needed minding without delay. He'd look up from whatever he was doing, when his ear caught the crunch of her feet on the road, and stand there, smiling at her, his face reddening, so that she felt no shame, no shyness, in smiling back freely. He was a year or two younger than her, but she'd have married him. She'd have gone to a dark field with him like she had with James, if the occasion had arisen. If he'd asked, if he'd been half as pushy as her groom had. And now he wouldn't be puking his guts out and sweating from wearing a straw boy's hat. He'd be wearing a suit that'd probably make him redden with shy pride.

Her mother had told her, when it became clear she was to marry James, that love was just a youthful fancy, just like wind, gone in a few years like a draught one closes a door against. Still, seeing Tom she felt a pinch in her chest. Had he changed, in the past year? Had men in the town taunted the softness out of him, had the O'Sheas of the world done their part, shaming him for leading a cushy life where roads were paved and people worked sitting down? Oonagh found it hard to imagine the soft boy she'd almost known would have willingly put on the straw hat.

When he'd finished emptying himself, Tom walked off to the wall that stood a few paces in the dark, coughing to get rid of the rottenness in his mouth, and sat down. Oonagh walked back inside, not looking at him, not knowing if he looked at her. By then it was quite late already, and you didn't need the hands of a clock to tell you so. The hands of the men were enough, their feet, their blood-filled faces, as if the drinks in their bellies had pushed all the blood outward. Their heads vile fleshy tumours on beer barrels.

The musicians had given up on slow numbers, and some guests seemed not to have left the dance floor in hours. They kept spinning, their sweat flying out in fat drops. At least everyone was too busy, or crazed, to notice her. She sat down on a bench along the wall, far enough from the buffet and the music that she could hope for peace for a little while.

She saw Uncle Mick on the dance floor, catching one of her bridesmaids by the hand. It was Louise, the Guiney girl. Uncle Mick spun her around roughly, and although Louise laughed at first along with the other guests who'd paused in their dancing to see what mischief Mick would be up to, soon her face hardened, and Oonagh wondered if she'd get sick. Then Uncle Mick stopped her suddenly, bringing her to him by grabbing her butt hard and pressing her against him. He released her after a second and freed her hand, having brought his booze-wet lips to it as if she were royalty. Her face was frozen as she walked away, but Oonagh saw Uncle Mick wink and laugh. She followed his gaze and saw the groom, James, her husband, sitting at a table and laughing with Mick.

O'Shea was sitting with him, along with a few other men. He had lifted the straw hat to rest on his forehead, so he could drink more easily, and he chatted with the others as if they were down at the pub, about cattle and silage and the Taoiseach's latest speech, she imagined. Weren't the straw boys supposed to stay hidden? To storm the party, and depart before their antics became boring?

"Some do, this, uh?" came a voice in her ear. Oonagh jumped, but a hand had come down and clamped her at the knee. She looked into the face, where a face should have been, but all she could see was straw. In the gaps between stalks, the dark seemed endless.

"So, little girl becomes woman. This is the way things go, uh? I'll let you on a little secret, though. It's not 'cause you're up the duff that you have to go and marry the actual amadán that knocked you up."

Oonagh sat frozen. The voice was unfamiliar, and without a mouth to connect it to, she felt like she wasn't even sure where it was coming from.

"Getting stiff is no big thing, girleen. That James of yours's nothing special. Pigs do it, y'know. Bees do it, surely you've heard that? Little bee hard-ons. Hive-wide humpings. Never heard meself of a bee proposing after an unfortunate fuck. No bee wedding. No straw bees to worry the little innocent bee bride's scrambled brains."

Oonagh managed to take her eyes off the straw head, and saw Claire, Louise, and Annie by the buffet, the world still going on beyond the darkness in the straw head, and she brushed off the straw boy's arm with the back of her hand. It lifted as if it weighed nothing.

After that she made sure not to be alone. She wasn't in the mood for all the small talk her friends and family reeled her into, the rejoicing, the inane congratulations, but at least she felt safe. She kept off the food and drinks—there was something at the pit of her stomach, something that hadn't been there before, that now pressed outward from her core as if it wished to burst her body open.

Soon all the food and drink was gone. Oonagh's mother had brought in an extra crate earlier on, but had then firmly denied the existence of any more. Oonagh could see her mother was happy now to see the night was winding down. Naggins appeared out of breast pockets, but those too were quickly drained, in

sneaky sips or generous rounds. People started heading off. Red faces converged to Oonagh, kissed her wetly, slurring congratulations that were more heartfelt than at the start of the night.

Then her friends started leaving, and Claire came to bid her farewell with a long embrace. James was still sitting at the table with O'Shea, who'd let the straw cone roll under the bench, and a couple of other men. They sat in drunk stupor, letting out exhausted snorts when one of them managed to come up with something to say and make his mouth say it. Oonagh's mother busied herself at the buffet, surveying what might be salvaged for the next day.

Then Oonagh saw him—the third straw boy. He was sitting there still, where he'd talked to her, where he'd put his hand on her knee, sitting there still like a bad joke. She felt an insatiable fury well up in her. She walked up to him; her teeth clenched with hatred.

"What do you think you're doing?"

He just sat there, not moving an inch, his unknowable face somewhere in there, his eyes maybe trained on her.

"Huh? Do you hear me?"

Her voice had risen, and she could feel in the periphery of her vision James and the men at the table looking at her. The straw cone was slightly askew on his shoulders, and she wondered if he'd fallen into a drinks-induced coma like James would do as soon as they reached their newlyweds' bed.

"All the booze's gone, so off with you!"

Oonagh clamped her hand on his shoulder and shook him like she wished she'd done earlier. The straw cone fell to the ground and rolled, empty, with a low rat-tat-tat on the concrete floor, and somehow the jacket and shirt collapsed into a pile of dirty laundry under her hand, the solidity she'd felt in her grip a second earlier all gone. She heard a tired laugh, but she couldn't be sure where it came from.

THE MACABRE READER

CʒƧꙨ

BOOK REVIEWS BY LYSETTE STEVENSON

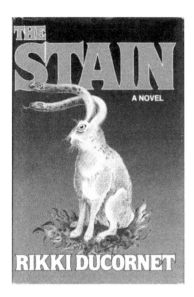

THE STAIN
by Rikki Ducornet.
Grove Press, 1984.

Set in a rural 1880s French village, Charlotte is born bearing a hare shaped birthmark on her face, branding her by the community as an outsider touched by witchcraft. Orphaned by the birthing death of her mother and the drinking death of her father she is taken underwing by a strict and miserly aunt and simple but doting uncle. After an incident where she deliberately consumes glass, her aunt, further convinced the birthmark is a sign of the devil, ships Charlotte off to a nunnery where she is pursued by a lecherous Exorcist. With supernatural happenings in the covenant and several hamlet children found butchered in the surrounding forest, a brigade sets off on a wolf hunt with Charlotte leading the pack.

This darkly comedic horror tale is observed through the eyes of Charlotte's innocent coming-of-age. The story is enhanced by Ducornet's oneiric narration, as she explores good and evil through the superstitious and ritualistic lives of the rural villagers. A wild ride of a novel, it was inspired by a series of dreams and synchronistic events Ducornet experienced during her time living in the Loire Valley.

An artist before a successful career as a novelist, Ducornet has never been bound by any one genre. This being her first novel, and while commonly classified as horror, it is likely to be shelved in the literary section of a used bookshop.

GHOSTLY TALES TO BE TOLD
edited by Basil Davenport.
Faber and Faber, 1953.

Ask any theatre practitioner and they will tell you among the most primal human experiences is gathering around a crackling fire and telling a good yarn. Even better if it raises the hackles a bit and causes the audience to grip the person opposite. Adrenaline and a little fear of the unknown is healthy for spirit and camaraderie.

Basil Davenport, a lover of strange tales and a theatre practitioner himself, sought to adapt his favourite ghost stories so they could be more readily shared within a group setting. While he arranges some of the more commonly found works of Weird Tales like Blackwood's "The Wendigo," Crawford's "The Screaming Skull," and Jacobs' "The Monkey's Paw." Included are rarer pieces such as Edward Lucas White's "The House of the Nightmare," where a man takes shelter in a haunted house. Jane Rice's "The Refugee," a werewolf tale in Nazi-occupied Paris and Manly Wade Wellman's, tense lockstep journey with two intrepid ghost hunters, "Where Angels Fear."

Davenport introduces this collection with an entertaining ten page essay On Story-Telling giving advice on how to host the readings, along with his process on how he chose to move things around for narrative effect. There is a beguiling quality to his enthusiasm of a well performed ghost tale that will make you want to gather your friends around and chill them to their bones.

TRIAD: A NOVEL OF THE SUPERNATURAL
by Mary Leader.
Book club edition Coward, McCann & Geoghegan, 1973.
Cover design, Paul Bacon.

After the loss of their infant, a couple relocates to a gothic manor perched on a cliffside above Lake Michigan. While the husband is frequently away on civil engineering work, his wife, Branwen, is left to renovate their new home with her loyal companion dog, Lance. Alone processing her grief and guilt, Branwen begins experiencing hauntings and blackouts. When she becomes pregnant again, her husband urges her into the care of an unorthodox psychiatrist. Combining elements of Welsh folklore with *The Yellow Wallpaper* and "The Tell-Tale Heart," *Triad* is an immersive, at times ghastly dive into an unreliable narrator with a remarkably dark ending.

Triad's notoriety is overly associated with Stevie Nicks. In a biographical anecdote Nicks claims she was so taken by the character name, Rhiannon, that it inspired what became one of Fleetwood Mac's biggest hits. Though she has asserted the creative urge was simply from the name alone; the witch-like lore that surrounds the bandmates' descriptions of Stevie being seemingly in a state of possession whenever she sang

"Rhiannon," mirrors back to the thematic elements of *Triad*. This book remains highly sought after by fans of the band.

THE DEMON LOVER
by Dion Fortune.
First print run, 1927.
Republished by Weiser books, 2010.
Cover illustration, Owen Smith.

Dion Fortune's first in a series of esoteric novels, *The Demon Lover* is a rip-roaring occult romance/thriller published in the same year as H. P. Lovecraft's *The Call of Cthulhu.*

A clairvoyant young woman takes a secretarial job for a wealthy and callous recluse. She soon finds herself bound to him by a psychic chain around her neck as his unconventional work requires her at his beck and call twenty-four hours a day. She begins

participating in trance seances where he uses her as a spy to infiltrate secrets from his former occult lodge. This lust for power and forbidden information sends both of them on the run from the elder occult order for meddling in their affairs. Psychic attacks, astral travel, etheric vampirism, animal possession and a battle of the mages. The tension in this horror novel mounts as unexpected plot twists lead to a final battle where the heroine comes into her own power.

Trained as a psychotherapist in England, Dion Fortune devoted herself to esoteric endeavors and the founding of her own occult lodge. A prolific writer of both fiction and nonfiction, her life was cut short by leukemia at the age of fifty-five.

THE NECRO NOM NOM NOM
written by Mike Slater.
Illustrated, Kurt Komoda.
Recipe tested, Tom Roache.

Published by Red Duke Games, 2019.

You won't find another functional cookbook that calls for anointed ichor purgings, fungoid vivisections, incantations, desecrations or the ravening diary entries of a multi-night bread pudding concoction. Recipe instructions that read "Ritual preparation... They are They shall ever be, They hunger. Let him who hath understanding, reckon the Number of the Beets, for it is a human number."

Printed in sepia, it appears like archeological field notes as well as a scrawling grimoire; Komoda's illustrations with Slater's handwritten recipes engulf each page. This gives the viewer an engaging art book and a somewhat practical cookbook once you decipher the 'offerings' through their Mythosian punnery. You will encounter "Innsmouth Shuck," "Moon-Beast Pies," "Tsathogguambalaja," and a "Pallid Bisque," where the recipe is broken down into theatrical acts. After the first edition they acknowledged feedback, wanting it to be a bit more accessible and the further print runs were expanded with formatted content to broaden its reach.

Personally, I find more charm in the cryptic nature of the Red Duke version, and despite the heavy presence of meat and sea creatures, a devout herbivore like myself, appreciates it for its high visual aesthetics and pitch-perfect wit. *The Necro Nom Nom Nom* brings a great deal of fun back into the kitchen, so dim the lights, don your cultist robes and prepare a feast for your monstrous friends - Iä! Iä!

Fall of 2021 they released the companion volume *Love-craft Cocktails: Elixirs & Libations from the Lore of H. P. Lovecraft.*

THREE MACABRE STORIES
by Rosaleen Norton.
The Teitan Press edition,
2010.
Cover painting from a private collection mural by Rosaleen Norton, circa 1940.

New Zealand born and Australian raised Rosaleen Norton was a notorious artist and iconoclast, dubbed 'The Witch of Kings Cross' by the press, referring to the part of Sydney's bohemia where she lived. In 1934, at the young age of fifteen and before establishing herself as an artist she wrote three short works of horror, all of which could've been in the pages of *Weird Tales*. Rosaleen brings to life a man obsessed with waxworks, finding himself trapped overnight in the museum. A morbid painter is driven mad by a ghoulish visage and two sisters rent a country cottage where they discover a sinister marble plinth in the orchard.

While playing with common tropes, the tales are well crafted and a delightful read. Having written them only in her mid-teens one wonders at the possibilities if she had focused her creative output on storytelling instead of painting. Especially as her iconic art vividly portrayed the phantasmagoria of occult imagery she could conjure. Sadly, she was far ahead of her time and police frequently harassed, confiscated and destroyed many of her works under the auspices of obscenity. The Teitan Press edition includes reproduc-tions of her artwork as well as two further short stories written by her then husband that undoubtedly bear a sense of her collaboration. Rosaleen Norton remains today a fasci-nating figure and finally, many years after her death, is receiving the recognition and respect she deserved.

WERWOLVES
by Elliott O'Donnell.
Longvue Press, 1965.
First published in 1912.

Elliott O'Donnell is best known as an Irish folklorist and ghost hunter. Here he gathers 'Werwolf' lore from around Europe with parts of Asia and Africa. While it is written to be a studious collection, it is also narrated anecdotally and with a flare that borders fiction. Regard-less, this work has largely influenced the contemporary canon of shapeshifter mythos.

O'Donnell zigzags across Europe from Spain to Siberia bringing together stories that could've been published in any horror anthology for their sense of immediacy, lurid atmospheres and potboiler pacing. The adjacent chapter on "Ghouls" tells a wonder-fully horrid tale of a bride to be in Brittany, who while playing with spiritualism is possessed by a ghoul spirit and then found feasting on the remains of her deceased mother-in-law. Or the Varg-amors of Sweden, old spinsters who dedicate them-selves to the care and feeding of werewolves in the dark forests. Contrary to the popular image of man changing into a fully formed wolf, much of Europe accounts the werwolf as solely bearing the head of a wolf on a human body.

Despite some reprehensibly imperialist viewpoints, this collection is an engaging read for those wanting to indulge in tales of haunted woodlands bearing lycanthropous waters and incandescent flowers. Stories are embellished with alchemical recipes, astronom-ical bearings and regional incantations giving it a sense he sat down with a notebook and tea in a witch's cottage. He captures the breathless terror in each of these stories as the discovery of a hungry wolf hunts each narrator down.

Whether authentically recorded from local villages and adorned by O'Donnell for entertainment's sake, *Werwolves* has left its mark on the popular lore of today.

THE BLACK SHIP
by Gerry William.
Theytus Books, 1994.

Considered the first indige-nous sci-fi novel published in Canada, Gerry William of the Splatsin nation explores themes of colonization and the Sixties Scoop, where indigenous children were forced into foster care, through a science fictional lens. Set in 2478 humankind is interstellar and freely traversing other planets and asteroids. The leading protag-onist is Enid Blue Starbreaker, a twice orphaned indigenous child taken in by the colonizing military and raised through their ranks despite being seen as the enemy or a slave class citizen. A mysterious black ship has appeared in the borderlands between two colonies, amor-phous in shape and indecipherable to modern technology. Exploratory missions are sent to make contact. Simultaneously, a haunted planet known to drive visitors insane is also

being scouted. Enid is torn between the culture that took her in after murdering her family, the people she shares her bloodline with, and the forces at play that are trying to weaponize her between them.

Gerry William weds his self-avowed trekkie fandom with indigenous philosophy and spirituality. Frequently the indigenous belief that everything is interconnected is repeated in the phrase "When I give to you, I give to myself." Here he creates a groundwork in which story-telling can explore future possibilities constructively and meaningfully.

In a recent conversation with Gerry, as he passed through our bookstore, he said the sequel to *The Black Ship* is still a possibility. I hope so, the wonders he created around the haunted planet and the ominous presence of the black ship left my imagination ignited.

Theytus Books is the oldest Indigenous publishing house in Canada having been estab-lished in 1980. It is located in the Sylix territory on the Penticton Indian Reserve in British Columbia.

ABERRANT VISIONS

∽∾

FILM REVIEWS BY TOM GOLDSTEIN

DON'T TELL A SOUL (2020)
Starring: Jack Dylan Grazer, Fionn Whitehead, Rainn Wilson, Mena Suvari
Director: Alex McAulay
Writer: Alex McAulay
Running time: 83 minutes

A man falls down a hidden well while chasing two teenage brothers who have robbed a house. The boys bicker over what to do about the man: help him or leave him. About half-way through there's a plot twist that adds a bit of moral shading to the dilemma. However, the movie

WANDER DARKLY (2020)
Starring: Sienna Miller, Diego Luna
Director: Tara Miele
Writer: Tara Miele
Running time: 97 minutes

A couple, whose relationship is on very shaky ground, is involved in a severe car crash. In the aftermath, they parse the details and meaning of their time together. Viewers may wonder if either, neither or both died or whether the narrative is dying thoughts, dreams, or live interaction. That doesn't really matter. It's the dissection of the relationship and the emotions involved that counts.

goes full python—as in snake, or maybe Monty—on itself, choking on Fionn Whitehead's performance as the elder brother and a gag-inducing climax involving the boys' ailing mother.

RENT-A-PAL (2020)
Starring: Brian Landis Folkins, Wil Wheaton, Amy Rutledge, Kathleen Brady
Director: Jon Stevenson
Writer: Jon Stevenson
Running time: 108 minutes

David is a lonely, unemployed 40-year-old who lives in his ailing mother's basement in 1990 and is her sole caregiver. He tries meeting women through video-taped profiles. He's unsuccessful but finds a connection after he picks up a tape called *Rent-A-Pal* and meets a guy named Andy who seems empathetic, always asks the right questions—and gets very jealous when David meets a real woman.

The movie is a different take on the imaginary-friend

genre. The performances are solid, but the film feels padded in the early parts, needlessly repetitive in the middle and the final act seems to come out of another movie. Viewers might want to think carefully about hanging out with this "friend."

MORTAL (2020)
Starring: Nat Wolff, Iben Akerlie, Per Frisch
Director: Andre Ovredal
Writers: Andre Ovredal, Norman Lesperance, Geoff Bussetil
Running time: 104 minutes

An injured backpacker limps into a Norwegian town and strange, destructive things happen. Based on Norse mythology and described by its director/co-writer as the anti-Marvel *Thor*, *Mortal* works as a so-so "origins" film—a sequel is being planned. But as a standalone movie, there's too much wrong with it. The first half-

hour is sluggishly paced, and later showdown scenes may induce a "why didn't they…?" especially from North American audiences. The scenery is great, however. In Norwegian, with English subtitles, and English.

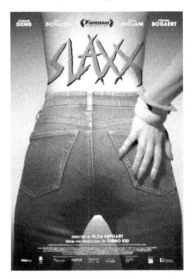

SLAXX (2020)
Starring: Romane Denis, Brett Donahue, Sehar Bhojani, et.al.
Director: Elza Kephart
Writers: Patricia Gomez, Elza Kephart
Running time: 77 minutes

You might remember *Killer Tomatoes*. How about trying on some "killer cotton." These jeans are a bit of a tight fit—and get tighter and tighter and tighter until they squeeze the life right out of you. Employees of an ultra-trendy apparel store find out the hard way in this largely satirical Canadian film of social commentary on a supposedly enlightened "sustainable" global industry that exploits its mostly youthful employees at the retail and—more significantly—manufacturing levels. Oh, and do enjoy the Bollywood-style dance of the denim.

HUNTER HUNTER (2020)
Starring: Camille Sullivan, Summer H. Howell, Devon Sawa, Nick Stahl
Director: Shawn Linden
Writer: Shawn Linden
Running time: 93 minutes

It is said that animals generally kill because they have to—to eat, to protect their families—while humans sometimes kill just because they can. In this Canadian thriller, a couple live off the land while homeschooling their daughter in the woods northeast of Winnipeg. Their existence is disrupted by the presence of a rogue wolf. But the canine isn't the only threat and a different type of beast emerges as the film shifts about two-thirds of the way through from a nerve-wrackingly tense thriller into a splatter-fest.

MY HEART CAN'T BEAT UNLESS YOU TELL IT TO (2020)
Starring: Patrick Fugit, Ingrid Sophie Schram, Owen Campbell.
Director: Jonathan Cuartas
Writer: Jonathan Cuartas
Running time: 90 minutes

A pair of adult siblings go to extreme lengths to provide sustenance for their frail, housebound younger brother whose biggest wish is to have the idyllic life he sees in the 1950s and '60s family shows he watches over and over again, just hanging out in the park with friends on sunny days. Fans of the Swedish vampire film *Let the Right One In* or its British-American remake *Let Me In* should

enjoy this low-key American gem.

ANYTHING FOR JACKSON (2020)
Starring: Sheila McCarthy, Julian Richings, Konstantina Mantelos
Director: Justin G. Dyck
Writer: Keith Cooper
Running Time: 97 minutes

A couple abducts a pregnant woman in a Satanic bid to resurrect their dead grandson. Director Justin G. Dyck puts his deep background in made-for-TV Christmas movies to good effect in this riff on Rosemary's Baby, keeping this film light without undermining its supernatural and horror elements. Fans of TV's *Murdoch Mysteries* can have some added fun trying to identify star Yannick Bisson here.

SHEEP WITHOUT A SHEPHERD (2019)
Starring: Yang Xiao, Zhuo Tan, Joan Chen, et. Al
Director: Sam Quah
Writers: Kaihua Fan, Sheng Lei, Peng Li, Yuqian Qin, Weiwei Yang, Pei Zhai
Running time: 112 minutes

An ordinary guy uses his encyclopedic knowledge of movie plotting to protect his family and stay ahead of police investigating the whereabouts of their chief's son. A bit sluggish at first, the movie picks up a breezy pace as the everyman goes up against a chief who is as brutal as she is brainy. A fun watch for those who enjoy Alfred Hitchcock movies.

GOODBYE HONEY (2020)
Starring: Pamela Jayne Morgan, Juliette Alice Gobin, et al.
Director: Max Strand
Writers: Max Strand, Todd Rawiszer
Running time: 95 minutes

A trucker taking a night-time break in an isolated state park encounters a young woman who claims to have escaped a kidnapper. What follows is a mostly lean—there's a red herring in the middle that's pretty obvious—talky tale of survival and trust. Some razzle dazzle editing and a nifty plot twist keep things moving along.

CONTRIBUTORS

☙☙

Annika Barranti Klein lives and writes in a tiny apartment in Los Angeles with her family and a collection of bones (mostly animal, mostly teeth). She likes stories about girls, monsters, and girls who are monsters. Her fiction has been in *Craft Literary, Hobart After Dark, Milk Candy Review, Mermaids Monthly*, and *Asimov's Science Fiction*. Find her online at annikaobscura.com.

Derrick Boden's fiction has appeared and is forthcoming in numerous venues including *Analog, Escape Pod*, and *Beneath Ceaseless Skies*. He is a writer, a software developer, an adventurer, and a graduate of the Clarion West class of 2019. He currently calls Boston his home, although he's lived in fourteen cities spanning four continents. He is owned by two cats and one iron-willed daughter. Find him at derrickboden.com and on Twitter as @derrickboden.

David Bowman's illustrations have appeared previously in *Weird Horror* and in *Field Notes from a Nightmare* from DreadStone Press. He lives in Fishers, Indiana with his family. David frequently posts new art on Twitter @dlbowman76, but please...don't hold that against him.

Armel Dagorn lives in Nantes with his wife and two kids, after having spent most of his twenties in Ireland. His short fiction has appeared and is forthcoming in such places as *Apex Magazine, Lamplight, Nightscript* and *The Shadow Booth*, as well as in the anthologies *Haunted Futures*, and *Strange California*. His short story collection *The Proverb Zoo* was published in 2018 by The Dreadful Press.

Sarina Dorie has sold over 180 short stories to markets like *Analog, Daily Science Fiction,*

The Magazine of Fantasy and Science Fiction, Fantasy Magazine, Orson Scott Card's Intergalactic Medicine Show, and *Abyss and Apex*. Her stories and published novels have won humor contests and Romance Writer of America awards. She has over seventy novels published, including her bestselling series, *Womby's School for Wayward Witches*. By day, Sarina is an art teacher, artist, belly dance performer and instructor, copy editor, fashion designer, event organizer and probably a few other things. By night, she writes. As you might imagine, this leaves little time for sleep. You can find info about her stories and novels on her website. Sign up for her newsletter to hear the latest news: www.sarinadorie.com

Daniel David Froid is a writer, scholar, and educator who lives in Indiana. His short fiction appears in *Coffin Bell, Ligeia*, and *Lightspeed*.

J.F. Gleeson is a writer residing in England. His work (fiction and otherwise) has appeared, or is soon to appear, in *Ligeia, Maudlin House, Dream Journal*, the *Bear Creek Gazette, Rejection Letters, The Daily Drunk, Overheard, Goat's Milk, Mandrake* and *Beneath Ceaseless Skies*. In the past, he has used the pen name John Banning. Find links to all his published work on his website: deadlostbeaches.blog

Tom Goldstein spent about 35 years working in various capacities in newsrooms of major newspapers across Canada—as a reporter, editor, and a couple of extracurricular stints as a music or video reviewer. He has never—and still does not—consider himself a critic. Rather he's just a guy who really likes movies, with a particular interest in "different."

Orrin Grey is a skeleton who likes monsters as well as the author of several spooky books. His stories of ghosts, monsters, and sometimes the ghosts of monsters can be found in dozens of anthologies, including Ellen Datlow's *Best Horror of the Year*. He resides in the suburbs of Kansas City and watches lots of scary movies. You can visit him online at orringrey.com.

Vince Haig is an illustrator, designer, and author. You can visit Vince at his website: barquing.com

Andrew Humphrey is the author of two collections of short stories, both published by Elastic Press. *Open the Box* appeared in 2002 and *Other Voices*, which was one of the winners of the inaugural East Anglian Book Award, in 2008. His debut novel, *Alison*, was published by TTA Press, also in 2008. His stories have appeared in magazines such as *The Third Alternative, Black Static, Crimewave, Bare Bone* and *Midnight Street*. He lives and works in Norwich in the UK and is currently working on another novel and short story collection.

Courtney Kelly is a freelance editor and layout designer. She's done editorial work for *TV Guide, On the Danforth Magazine*, and Undertow Publications, among others.

Our cover artist, **Drazen Kozjan**, is the creator of *The Happy Undertaker* comic strip. instagram.com/drazenkozjan

Linda Niehoff is a photographer and a nostalgist with a penchant for silver water towers at dusk, ghost stories, and a collection of old Polaroid cameras. Her short fiction can be found or is forthcoming in *The Magazine of Fantasy & Science Fiction, Flash Fiction Online, TriQuarterly*, and elsewhere. Find her intermittently on twitter: @lindaniehoff

Lysette Stevenson is a stage manager with a rural outdoor equestrian theatre company and a second-generation bookseller. She lives in British Columbia.

Ashley Stokes is the author of *Gigantic* (Unsung Stories, 2021), *The Syllabus of Errors* (Unthank Books, 2013) and *Voice* (TLC Press, 2019), and editor of the *Unthology* series and *The End: Fifteen Endings to Fifteen Paint-*

ings (Unthank Books, 2016). His recent short fiction appears in *Black Static; Nightscript; The Ghastling; Out of Darkness* (edited by Dan Coxon, Unsung Stories), and *This is Not a Horror Story* (edited by JD Keown, Night Terror Novels). Other stories have appeared in *Tales from the Shadow Booth Vol. 4, BFS Horizons, Bare Fiction, The Lonely Crowd, the Warwick Review, Storgy* and more. He is currently working on *The Underkin and Other Stories*, a short story sequence that includes *Fields and Scatter*. He lives in the East of England where he's a ghostwriter and ghost.

Simon Strantzas is the author of five collections of short fiction, including *Nothing is Everything* (Undertow Publications, 2018), and editor of a number of anthologies, including *Year's Best Weird Fiction, Vol. 3*. He is the co-founder and associate editor of the irregular journal, *Thinking Horror*, and, combined, has been a finalist for four Shirley Jackson Awards, two British Fantasy Awards, and the World Fantasy Award. His fiction has appeared in numerous annual best-of anthologies, and in venues such as *Nightmare, The Dark,* and *Cemetery Dance*. In 2014, his edited anthology, *Aickman's Heirs*, won the Shirley Jackson Award. He lives with his wife in Toronto, Canada.

Steve Rasnic Tem, a past winner of the Bram Stoker, World Fantasy, and British Fantasy Awards, has published 470+ short stories. Recent collections include *The Night Doctor & Other Tales* (Centipede) and *Thanatrauma: Stories* (Valancourt). His novel *Ubo* is a dark science fictional tale about violence and its origins, featuring such viewpoint characters as Jack the Ripper and Stalin. *Yours to Tell: Dialogues on the Art & Practice of Writing*, written with his late wife Melanie, is available from Apex Books. You can visit his home on the web at www.stevetem.com.

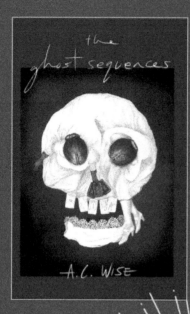

UNDERTOW PUBLICATIONS

Lightning Source UK Ltd.
Milton Keynes UK
UKHW050842070822
406948UK00007B/591